"If You'd Behaved Better," Angelo Said, "You Might Not Be In This Predicament."

Surely Angelo wasn't suggesting they might still be together? Not when Gemma knew the kind of man he was. A playboy. A man who traded one beautiful woman for another, as soon as her sell-by date was over.

Her lip curled. "You mean if I were still your mistress? Putting up with your demands, your—"

"I thought you'd forgotten everything. So how do you remember how demanding I was?" His tone held sensual rasp, belied by his shrewd gaze. He reached out and put a finger under her chin. He put enough pressure to tilt her head up, so that he could stare down into her eyes.

The sudden flare of heat that followed in the wake of the touch of that one finger shocked her. No. He was the last man on earth to whom she could afford to be attracted.

A spoiled playboy who'd had a fortune handed to him on a plate. A dilettante who destroyed without compunction.

"You tempt me to prove you a liar," he said.

Dear Reader,

As a teenager I read romances that I discovered in the garage...and later in the library and bookshops. There were all sorts of stories. Reunion stories, stranded at sea stories, secret baby stories...some of them seemed quite far-fetched to me. But it didn't matter how unrealistic a story might be, I finished it to discover the happy ending.

In those days I used to horse ride a lot. I'm told one day I fell off a horse—I don't remember. Or rather I remember getting onto the nag early that morning. It had been giving me a little bit of trouble and I was supposed to sort it out—well, three hours later I was in hospital, lights out. I came round the next morning with a killer headache. The funny part of it all is that the guy who saw me fall off and who called my mom, summoned help and did all the things a hero should is now my husband—and I don't remember the first time we ever met.

Every time I fell off a horse afterward, I waited for the jolt to bring my memory back, like in romances I'd read—it never did. But I still got my happy ending!

I hope you enjoy *The Apollonides Mistress Scandal*. Please visit me at my Web site www.tessaradley.com to find out more about my upcoming books. I always love hearing from readers!

Take care

Tessa

TESSA RADLEY

THE APOLLONIDES MISTRESS SCANDAL

Published by Silhouette Books
America's Publisher of Contemporary Romance

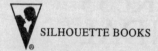

SILHOUETTE BOOKS

ISBN-13: 978-0-373-76829-5
ISBN-10:   0-373-76829-X

THE APOLLONIDES MISTRESS SCANDAL

Books by Tessa Radley

Silhouette Desire

Black Widow Bride #1794
Rich Man's Revenge #1806
The Kyriakos Virgin Bride #1822
The Appolonides Mistress Scandal #1829

*Billionaire Heirs

TESSA RADLEY

loves traveling, reading and watching the world around her. As a teen Tessa wanted to be an intrepid foreign correspondent. But after completing a bachelor of arts and marrying her sweetheart, she became fascinated with law and ended up studying further and practising as an attorney in a city law firm.

A six-month break traveling through Australia with her family re-awoke the yen to write. And life as a writer suits her perfectly; traveling and reading count as research and as for analyzing the world...well, she can think *what if* all day long. When she's not reading, traveling or thinking about writing she's spending time with her husband, her two sons—or her zany and wonderful friends. You can contact Tessa through her Web site www.tessaradley.com.

ACKNOWLEDGMENTS

To the readers on the eHarlequin.com
10,000 Book Challenge boards. You blew my annual
book budget in about a month!:-) But I thank each one of
you for the great recommendations and lots of fun.

To Melissa Jeglinski, my thanks
for valued advice and thanks to Karen Solem
for always being there for me. And Abby, Karina
and Sandra, what would I do without you?

To my family—
Tony, Alex and Andrew, you guys are simply the best!

One

Gemma Allen was back.

Forcing himself to snap out of the shock that held him rigid, Angelo Apollonides strode across the pale sand towards the woman who had betrayed him.

His staff had not lied. The nasty truth was that his beautiful former mistress stood on *his* beach, on *his* island admiring one of *his* sleek, double-hulled catamarans. And Angelo intended to find out precisely why she had chosen to return.

"What are you doing here?" Angelo fought to keep his voice even, to keep the string of ugly curses from escaping. "I never expected to see you again. Particularly not here on Strathmos."

She turned, her tawny eyes wide and startled. The first week of November had passed, the evenings on

Strathmos had begun to cool. The sea wind caught at Gemma's dark red hair, whipping it across her face, hiding her expression for a beat of time. When she brushed it back, she'd recovered her equilibrium and her eyes were wary.

"Angelo." Gemma's voice was cool, composed. A world away from the alarm that had flickered in her eyes only seconds before. "How are you?"

"Forget the pleasantries. You have nerve showing up at the Palace of Poseidon." Angelo pressed his mouth into a tight, forbidding line. "I couldn't believe it when I was told you are performing in the Electra Theatre."

She shrugged. "It's a free world. I can work where I want."

"Anywhere except on Strathmos. This is my world, run by my rules." The island was more than his world; it was his home. The resort had been created from his dreams. Today he'd returned after a hectic month away to find that Gemma had already been working here for over a week.

"Do you really want to be faced with an unfair-dismissal action?" Her wariness had been replaced with attitude.

Angelo froze. He was known to be a fair employer, hard but just. He didn't need the headache of an industrial action—and there was a good chance she'd succeed. Frustrated, he stared at the face that had grown more beautiful in the years since they'd been apart. Her hair was longer…wilder, her eyes glowed brighter and as for her mouth…that lush red mouth taunted him with fighting words. He jerked his attention away from her provocative mouth and gave her slender body an insultingly slow once-over. "Singer is certainly a step up from exotic dancer."

"It's been three years. Things change," she pointed out.

"*I* haven't changed." He widened his stance and put his hands on his hips.

"No, you haven't changed one little bit," she agreed.

He assessed her through slitted eyes, not liking the bite in her tone. "So what do you want, Gemma? A second chance?"

An emotion he couldn't decipher flitted across her stunning features. Gemma gave a brittle laugh. "A second chance? With you? You must be mad!"

He frowned, not liking the fact that he couldn't read her any longer. "Why are you here?"

"I'm here to work…it's a free world." With a sweeping hand she gestured to the blue stretch of the Aegean Sea beyond the beach where the catamarans rested. "You—or rather your minions—gave me the job. The money was too good to pass up."

"Aah. Money."

"Don't scorn the lack of it so easily." Her eyes were flashing now. "Just because you inherited an empire of resorts that stretch across the Greek isles before you turned twenty-one doesn't give you the right to look down your nose at me. I need the money."

Angelo felt himself bristle. Her tongue had developed a razor-sharp edge since their last unforgettable encounter. "I worked damn hard to build a chain of family hotels into world-class resorts. And you never objected to the funds it gave you access to in the past."

He felt her withdraw, even before her eyes went blank. Then she murmured, "If the recent tabloids are to be believed, you're so far removed from us ordinary working mortals, you might as well inhabit Mount Olympus."

"You should know better than to believe everything you read in the newspapers," he snapped, shuddering at the memory of the latest batch of headlines about his breakup with Melina.

"Really?" She raised an eyebrow. "You're not the playboy they portray you to be? You don't wear a different rising starlet or supermodel on your arm every month?"

He glared at her, his frustration increasing to a rising inferno, fanned by her sharp words. "The media exposure is advantageous to both the women and myself."

"So it's all about glamour? About creating an illusion about the rich and famous, then? Nothing more?"

His brows jerked together. "Why are you so interested—unless you do want a chance to get back into my bed?"

She snorted. "I don't want you back."

His mouth slanted. "Didn't anyone tell you that you should be nice to the boss? Three years ago you would've never dared speak to me as you just did."

"Three years ago, I was a silly little goose."

She shifted and her tank top rode up, revealing a strip of tanned midriff. Every male instinct went on alert. "But you don't deny that you are interested?" Angelo moved closer.

Gemma glanced at her watch. "I can't deny you're a fascinating man."

The bite was back. He gave a surprised laugh. "You don't want me back…but you're interested enough to admit you find me fascinating? What message are you trying to send me?"

For an instant she looked rattled. He noticed that goose bumps had risen on her arms. "Are you cold?"

"No." She rubbed her arms briskly, not meeting his eyes.

He touched her arm where the fine hairs stood on end. Gently. With a fingertip. "If you are not cold, then what is this?"

She jerked away. Her gaze swung up to meet his. He read bewilderment...and something more. A stark, turbulent emotion. Fear?

Gemma stepped away. "Excuse me." The smile she gave him didn't reach the eyes that were stretched wide. "But I need to go. It's nearly time for the show. I've got to get ready. Maybe you can come watch." She flung the invitation over her shoulder. As she brushed past him, Angelo let the weight of his hand land on her arm, stilling her.

She turned. This time, he was certain of the emotion that darkened her eyes from tawny to a deep sherry-brown.

It *was* fear. Powerful and totally overwhelming. He inspected her. From close-up he took in her darkened eyes, the taut tension in her face, the tiny shivers that rippled across her skin. He could smell the saltiness of the sea in her hair and feel the cool edge of the wind on her skin.

Why was she here? She'd implied she needed money. Was that the only reason? Or, despite her denial, did she hope to rekindle the burnt-out embers of their affair?

"Let me go." Her voice was toneless. Pointedly, she stared at his long, tanned fingers lying against her skin.

He removed them, taking his time and watching intently as she hauled in a steadying breath.

The nagging wind tugged at her wayward hair as she gave a hurried glance at her watch and scooped up the sandals lying in the sand. "I suppose I should say it's been nice seeing you—"

"But you'd be lying."

"I didn't say that." She stilled. There was chagrin in her eyes. "Don't put words in my mouth."

Her mouth. His gaze dropped to her rosy lips. Full and lush. The sudden surge of desire was unexpected. It left him reeling. He clenched his fists. How could he want Gemma Allen? After everything she'd done?

How the hell could he have forgotten how sexy she was? The lush bee-stung lips, the sinuous curves of her sleek body, the cloud of dark red hair…how could he have let those details slide from his consciousness?

Reluctant to examine the discovery that he still desired her, he said softly between his teeth. "From exotic dancer into singer…I want to see this transformation. I'll be at your show."

Half an hour later, wearing only lacy briefs and a silky black halter-neck slip, Gemma sat alone in front of the mirror in the dressing room she shared with Lucie LaVie, a likeable comedienne who did a very funny routine in the bar adjacent to the Electra Theatre.

Meeting Angelo on the beach so unexpectedly had been a shock. Dammit, she hadn't even known he was back. She'd been on Strathmos for just over a week, waiting for him, half-dreading their first encounter. She'd planned to be prepared…to be dressed to the nines…to show him what he was missing when they met again. Instead she'd been wearing shorts, no make-up and her legs had been covered in sand. She certainly hadn't expected the curious numbness that had enveloped her.

Staring into the mirror, Gemma couldn't help wondering what Angelo would make of the transformation. The heavy stage makeup gave her skin an unnatural perfection, blotting out the light sprinkle of freckles across her nose and cheeks. Eyeliner accentuated her tawny eyes and dark ruby lipstick added lushness to her lips that gave her an in-your-face sensuality.

Angelo liked his women beautiful and flamboyant. His most recent mistresses had all been actresses or famous models. And, according to the recent tabloids she'd studied, he still showed no sign of settling down. She examined herself in the mirror. She looked beautiful…flamboyant. And Angelo would be out there tonight watching her.

Her plan had to—

A rap on the door broke into her desperate thoughts. "Ten minutes to showtime, Gemma."

"Won't be long," she called back, and ran her fingers through her hair in an effort to tame the wild auburn curls. She couldn't remember the last time a man's fingers had stroked through them. A vivid image of Angelo's hand on her arm, his long fingers and buffed square nails, flashed into her mind and she swore softly.

An instant later the door burst open and Angelo entered with all the force and energy of a hurricane.

"Hey. You can't come in here!" After the initial shock, Gemma resisted the urge to cross her hands over her breasts. Despite the skimpy fabric and the low dip in the front, the slip covered all the strategic places.

Angelo shut the door and, folding his arms, leaned against it. "There's nothing to see that I haven't seen before."

Right. Gemma swallowed. Then she let her gaze run over him. He looked magnificent. The white dinner jacket must've been tailored to fit his tall body. Under the lights, his hair gleamed like old gold and his startling turquoise eyes blazed. He looked assured, wealthy, powerful.

And this was the man she intended to teach a lesson he'd never forget.

"What do you want?"

"Join me in the theatre for a drink after the show."

Gemma hid her exultation. It had been worth coming all the way to Strathmos. A few years ago he would've impressed her—with his Greek-god looks and the sheer force of his personality. But these days she didn't go for the domineering masterful type.

She dared not give in too quickly. She didn't want to lose his interest. Nor could she let herself forget for one moment why she was doing this.

"Don't you think you should wait outside until I am dressed?" Gemma waited a beat then added delicately, "Boss…"

Angelo's brows jerked into a frown at her disparaging tone and Gemma felt a fierce rush of pleasure. Of course, he was accustomed to admiration…adulation… women falling all over him. But not her.

"You—" He broke off and sucked in a deep breath. Then in a soft, dangerous tone, he said, "Do not presume on our past relationship."

"I would never do that." In the mirror, she slanted him a small smile. "I came to Palace of Poseidon to sing."

"Precisely." He didn't smile back. His eyes were bright and ruthless. "Or were you lying earlier? Perhaps you *were* hoping I'd want you back in my bed?"

Annoyance swarmed through Gemma. Quickly, she veiled her gaze before he glimpsed her ire. "I never imagined you'd want that. And nor do I. I've told you that already." Gemma drew a steadying breath. She had to be very careful; she could mess it all up with one careless mistake.

"I thought you might be hankering after the style to which you'd become accustomed."

God, he was arrogant. Gemma spun around on the plastic stool and glared up at Angelo. He was so tall, he positively loomed over her. "You make me sound like a sycophant. I worked for you, as well."

"You consider sharing my bed for half a year work?" The look he gave her stripped her naked of the silky slip and told exactly how little respect Angelo had for her.

Again, she fought the urge to cover her breasts, to check that the silky material didn't reveal the outline of her dark nipples. Supremely self-conscious now, she rose and crossed to the corner of the room where a small closet held several outfits.

Gemma peeled the dress she intended wearing tonight off its hanger. Keeping her back firmly to Angelo, she slid on the sleek crimson tube covered with winking sequins that should have clashed terribly with her hair but didn't.

The electrifying quality of the silence behind her flustered her. Gemma swivelled. The expression in Angelo's eyes made her breath catch. She became aware that the dress hugged her curves like a lover, that the neckline was low, provocative. That she and Angelo were totally alone.

Hurriedly she said, "My career has always been important to me." And fame had been important, too, she supposed.

"If you say so." He gave her a strange, intent look. "I say that changed once you got what you wanted…"

"And what do you think I wanted?" Then wished the words unsaid as tension sparked in the air between them. Suddenly Gemma didn't want to know the answer.

A frown drew his surprisingly dark brows together. "A man wealthy enough to pander to your every whim. A gold card with no ceiling…clothes, jewellery…" His gaze dropped pointedly to the gold ring set with a large showy topaz on the little finger of her left hand. "You chose that after we visited Monaco for a weekend. Remember?"

"I'm afraid I don't." She grabbed a pair of gloves out the closet and, with an ease born of practice, pulled on the long, black lace gloves embroidered with dark red roses and covered the ring. Outside the door, Mark Lyme, the manager of the entertainment centre called her name. Gemma moved towards the door. "I must go, I'm due on stage."

"Wait, you're not running out on this conversation." Angelo flung his hands out wide. "Of course you remember. That night we attended the Rose Ball, and you wanted to go partying afterwards. You flirted with every man who glanced your way."

Men? She hesitated. *What men?* "No—"

"Were there so many men that you cannot remember the one from the other?" Angelo's eyes glittered.

"I don't remember—"

"Oh, please, don't feed me that. You're wearing that ring *I* bought and paid for. Did I buy you so much jewellery that you can no longer remember the occasion of each purchase? I'm sure you remember every moment of the time we spent in bed afterwards."

Gemma's stomach turned. Outside, Mark called again. Gemma wrenched open the dressing-room door. "That's just it," she cut in before Angelo could interrupt again. "I don't remember. Nothing about that night at the Rose Ball. Nothing about you. Nothing about our time together. I've lost my memory."

Gemma bolted out onto the dimly lit stage, the vision of Angelo's stunned expression imprinted on her mind. She stared blindly out at the audience. She had to get a grip. She had to thrust the disturbing scene in the dressing room with Angelo out of her mind.

The chatter stilled and the cutlery stopped clinking. By now most of the patrons had finished their meal. Being Friday night, the supper theatre was packed. Gemma paused. Clouds from the smoke machine swirled around her, coloured by red and blue lighting and adding to the moodiness.

For a moment the familiar nervousness swept her. Then she embraced it and stepped forward to the waiting crowd. This was a space she cherished, a special place where her voice and mind and body all flowed into the music.

It was at the close of the second song that she spotted Angelo through the feathers of smoke. He sat alone at a table, casually propped against the wall, his arm along the back of the chair. The narrowed gaze focused on her revealed nothing. And the table in front of him was empty of food or drink.

Gemma quaked at the prospect of joining him for the drink he'd invited her for. The memory of how her skin had prickled when he'd touched her and the blind fear that had followed, swept over her.

Ripping her attention away from him, Gemma worked to make the crowd smile…and sigh. As her voice died after the final held note of the last song there was a moment's silence, then clapping thundered through the theatre. Gemma blew them two-handed kisses and sank into a bow, her unruly hair sweeping forward. She straightened and flicked her hair back and the clapping evolved into stamps and whistles.

"All right, one more, an Andrew Lloyd Webber composition, a personal favourite," she agreed. Her voice reverberated and the cacophony subsided. "If you've ever lost a loved one, this one is for you."

Gemma launched into "Memory." Her voice cut through the theatre, sharp and pure. She barely noticed that the audience seemed to hold its collective breath and when she reached the last line she let the final notes slide into silence.

This time the crowd went mad.

Smiling, Gemma waved to them. But she couldn't stop her gaze seeking Angelo's. The lyrics lingered in her mind. *A new day.* For a long moment their eyes held, the connection taut, and her smile faded.

There would be no new day for them. The past lay between them like an unassailable barrier.

Gemma was trembling with reaction by the time she reached the dressing room. She felt as if she'd been two rounds with Rocky Balboa. Lucie had returned from her act and lay sprawled along the length of the two-seater couch, dressed in funky street clothes that suited her spiky blonde hair and wide eyes.

"Boss wants to see you," she said, tossing a slip of paper into the trash basket as Gemma sat down.

"Mark?"

"No, the big fish, Angelo Apollonides." Lucie's green eyes were curious. "A reminder that you're to join him for a drink at his table. You didn't say anything about that invitation."

Gemma should have known that he wouldn't let her get away. That he'd want to know more about the bomb-shell she'd dropped before she had rushed out.

"It happened just before the show." Gemma wasn't confessing that Angelo had been here, in the dressing room. And she'd never told Lucie anything—thankfully no one had commented on the past affair. Perhaps most of the entertainment staff had only been there less than two years. "I'm too dog-tired to cope with Mr. Apollonides," Gemma muttered. The fatigue was not physical. It went soul-deep. She felt raw and emotionally drained. And she couldn't face Angelo right now.

The memory of how she'd reacted to his touch had spooked her. The last thing she needed was to feel desire for Angelo Apollonides. She needed time to come to terms with that unexpected complication. When she confronted Angelo it would be in her space, on her terms, not in the dark smoky intimacy of the supper theatre.

At Lucie's look of blatant disbelief, Gemma added, "And you can tell him that I'm passing for now." Rejection would do Angelo the world of good. Make him more eager to see her again.

"Gemma, you're being stupid. In the eight months I've been working on Strathmos he's never once invited an employee for a drink. And you refuse?" Lucie jumped up and started pacing the small space. "I just don't get you. He didn't even bring a woman with him to Strathmos this time, rumour has it that he ended it with—" she named a well-known model "—last month. Why not try your luck?"

Gemma didn't answer. She picked up a bottle of makeup remover and a packet of face wipes and started to clean her face with quick, practised moves. Soon Angelo would come looking for her, and she had no intention of being here.

After a moment Lucie gave a snort of disgust and stalked out of the room, muttering something about being the messenger of bad tidings and that some people had all the luck.

But Gemma knew Angelo's demand to join him had nothing to do with luck. His reaction on the beach had made it clear he was less than happy about her appearance on Strathmos.

She had to play this very, very carefully. For a year she'd been trying to get close to him. She'd finally been granted a four-week chance when the performer who was originally booked had pulled out. Gemma's agent had scrambled for the booking. With only eighteen days left to discover what she wanted and find a way to make Angelo pay for the grief he'd caused her, she couldn't chicken out just because her senses had been set on fire by the touch of a single finger.

Two

Gemma had stood him up!

And she hadn't even bothered to tell him herself, she'd sent a messenger to deliver the unwelcome news. The anger that had simmered within Angelo since he'd that discovered Gemma was on Strathmos, living and working in *his* resort, took on a new edge.

Gemma claimed that she'd lost her memory. How had that happened and what did it have to do with him? And why had she returned to Strathmos?

Angelo found himself glaring in the direction where the maddeningly capricious Gemma had vanished from the stage, while the bare skin of her back and that provocative red dress remained imprinted on his vision. He hated the sneaky realisation that he hadn't stopped thinking about her since he'd arrived back on

Strathmos. And now she'd deliberately left him cooling his heels.

Angelo rose to his feet, abandoning the bottle of Bollinger he'd ordered—Gemma had always had a taste for champagne—and, jaw set, stalked out to find her.

She was not in the dressing room. But a comprehensive scan took in the red dress hanging in the closet. Clearly, she'd already been and gone. Nor was she to be found in the row of bars and coffee shops that flanked the theatre. Angelo barely slowed his long strides as Mark Lyme hurried over. Two minutes later, with the next potential crisis averted, he exited the entertainment complex, searching for Gemma's distinctive dark flame hair under the lamps in the wide paved piazza.

About to veer off to where the staff units were located, he spotted a lone figure walking towards the deserted beach. Hunching his shoulders against the rising wind, Angelo quickened his pace. With her give-away hair, not even the fact that she wore jeans and a bulky sweater could hide that it was Gemma.

He came up behind her. "If I give an employee an order I expect it to be obeyed." The deceptive softness of his tone didn't hide his anger—or his frustration.

Gemma's shoulders tensed and she came to a halt. Then she turned. In the dim light of the lanterns that lined the promenade, he saw her eyebrow arch. "I thought it was an invitation," she said with soft irony. "One that I never accepted."

"Or refused."

She considered him, her head on one side. "Give me one good reason why I should have joined you."

He blinked. Women usually thronged to his side.

Hell, he didn't need to issue invitations. Women gate-crashed celebrity functions to meet him. "Because I wanted to speak to you."

"What about?" Her tension was tangible.

"Your memory loss."

"Not true. You invited me for a drink before you knew about that."

She had him there. What he really wanted to know was why she had come back to Strathmos. It had to be about more than money. His gut told him it had something to do with her amnesia. He wasn't about to admit that what pricked his ego was the fact that she didn't remember him. Or was it a ploy? Was her amnesia nothing more than a sham designed to avoid facing up to her treachery three years ago? Or a last-ditch effort to recapture his interest? At last he said, "You've forgotten carrying on with every male under the age of eighty at the Rose Ball? You don't remember about me…us?"

She closed her eyes at the sheer incredulity in his voice. "Is that so hard to accept?" she asked warily. "I have amnesia."

"How convenient."

Gemma opened her eyes and met his narrowed gaze. She tried to speak but her voice wouldn't work. So she simply shrugged and let her arms fall uselessly by her side.

"What kind of amnesia?"

"Does it matter?" The sick feeling in the pit of her stomach tightened. Couldn't he see how much she hated this? "Fact is, I can't remember anything about what happened here three years ago. It's just…one vast blank."

"It certainly explains how you have the gall to come back."

She let that barb go. "It's not easy being here. But I need to find out about my life. What it was like… well…before." She slid him a sideways look. The anger had faded, but his eyes still glittered with suspicion. "It's really strange, because I remember lots of stuff before I met you. Most of it, I think. And I know what happened…afterwards. It's the time in the middle that's gone."

He loomed over her. "How did it happen? Did you fall? Did you hit your head? What do the doctors say about the prognosis? Will you ever get that part of your memory back?"

"I don't know. I don't want to talk about it." Gemma's voice sounded thin and thready even to her own ears. "It upsets me."

Angelo gave a harsh sigh. "I suppose I can understand that. It must be scary."

Not as scary as Angelo. Even when he was being nice—like now, when his eyes were full of sympathy—there was a taut purpose to his body, an air of danger and tension. Gemma shuddered. Nice wouldn't last. Not with Angelo Apollonides. He hadn't transformed a string of family resorts into modern extravaganzas built for year-round entertainment by being a nice, sympathetic kind of guy. He was tough, decisive and ruthless. A man who worked hard—and played harder. A Greek success legend.

His gaze was direct. "Have dinner with me."

The unexpected request startled her. She chewed her lip. It was what she ought to do.

"Is it such a difficult decision? Do I scare you so much?" His hands came down on her shoulders and the touch scorched straight through her lamb's-wool sweater.

She went very still. "You don't scare me at all," Gemma said with false bravado.

His hands tightened. "Prove it by having dinner with me."

A dare. How infantile. She froze under his touch. A hint of stubble darkened his jaw and the hard line of his mouth had relaxed into a sensual curve. The dark intensity of his gaze and the way her flesh reacted to his touch told her that he was way out of her league. She wasn't ready to have dinner with him, to be the sole focus of his attention. He was so much more than she'd expected. But she had no choice. Not if she wanted to learn what she needed. "Not tonight. It's been a long day. And it's late."

He was about to say something, to argue, when his cell phone trilled. He mouthed an apology and turned away, talking rapidly in Greek, and Gemma realised she'd lost his attention.

Gemma wanted to kick something—preferably herself—and she wished desperately she'd accepted his invitation. Even though the prickles of excitement his touch had generated terrified her.

He hit a button and slid the phone into his pants pocket. "Tomorrow night?"

Relief overwhelmed her. She hadn't blown it. She drew a deep, shuddering breath. "Okay, I'll have dinner with you."

"So how did we meet?" The following evening Gemma sat across from Angelo in a secluded corner of the Golden

Fleece restaurant, her half-eaten meal of grilled calamari garnished with sliced lemon in front of her.

"At the film festival in Cannes." Angelo set down his knife. His plate was empty. "I thought you were an actress."

That would explain some of it. Angelo had never been linked with a dancer previously.

"Oh? What happened next?" She speared another tube of calamari and popped it into her mouth.

"You were beautiful—and funny. I enjoyed your company so I invited you to spend a weekend at Poseidon's Cavern." He named one of the famous resorts that he owned. "You accepted. And, when business called, you came back to Strathmos with me—it's where I live, after all." He gave her a grin that transformed his face, the harsh line of his mouth softening into a passionate curve.

Gemma set her knife and fork together and shifted in her chair, uncomfortable with the notion that it had been so easy for him. "And then I got a job in the resort? Right?"

"Do you want desert?"

"No, thanks."

"Coffee?"

She shook her head, impatient for his answer to her questions.

He came around and pulled out her chair. Close to her ear he murmured, "There was so much more glamour in being the boss's girlfriend than working." His voice was loaded with cynicism. "And you'd led me to believe you were taking a break from stage work. I had no idea you were an exotic dancer until about a month later."

"Oh." Gemma rose and shot him a wary glance. "I never wanted to…leave?"

He gave a hard-edged grin. "Why should you have? You had it all. Great resorts to live in, an unending credit line and good sex."

That was supposed to be funny? Gemma had never felt less like laughing in her life. She walked quickly ahead, not noticing the attractive man with long dark hair who waved to her. She smouldered silently until they exited the restaurant.

"So I no longer had a career—" She squawked in shock as Angelo pulled her into an alcove behind an immense bronze statue of Hephaestus. The sconce of fire that burned in the statue's raised hand cast leaping shadows against the walls. Gemma opened her mouth to protest.

"If you mean, you no longer danced half naked in an upmarket bar, then no, you no longer had a career. Instead you had me." In the close confines of the alcove his face had changed, toughened. He looked hard and ruthless and suddenly Gemma could see exactly why he was such a successful businessman and commanded so much respect. She had to take care not to provoke him.

"I had you." Gemma struggled to keep the anger at his arrogance out of her voice. "And what did you get out of this deal?"

"A beautiful woman in my bed."

"I don't suppose it occurred to you I might've wanted more?"

"More?"

"A career—"

He gave a snort. "You scored by being my live-in

lover. Travel to different resorts. A-list parties. No need to work. Believe me, it was better for you my way."

His way. Gemma had a feeling that most things ended up his way. The alternative would be for his kept mistress to hit the highway. "Did you love *me?*"

"Love you?" His head went back and she could see she'd surprised him.

"Yes, did you love me?" She pressed. "With all this good sex, did you feel anything for me at all?"

"Look, Gemma, this wasn't about love. It was about two consenting adults who met and enjoyed time together." He spread his hands sideways. "Hell, we were hardly Romeo and Juliet."

"If we had been Romeo and Juliet, you'd have been dead by the end," Gemma said through gritted teeth.

"Hey," he objected, "what are you getting so worked up about? All I meant was that we weren't young lovers, dizzy from an attack of first-time love."

"Did *I* love *you?*"

He gave an astonished laugh. "What's the fixation with love? You certainly never told me you loved me. But then you weren't in it for love. And nor was I."

Gemma bit her lip, thinking furiously. "I can't believe I would've lived the kind of life you've painted for any other reason than because I loved you more than anything in the world. It's so against everything I believe in."

"Well, you showed no sign of loving me…and if that's what you believe now, then you've changed."

She stilled. "Maybe I have."

His eyes darkened. "Gemma." He stretched out a hand and stroked her arm. "You should—"

"What am I doing?" She dropped her face into her hands, then raked her fingers back through her hair.

"Trying to regain your memory? Maybe this will help you remember." There was a huskiness to his voice that caught her attention.

Slowly she raised her head. He was close, far closer than she'd realised and in the flickering light his gaze was intent. Her heart started to pound. She swallowed and the sudden ringing silence stretched between them.

"Yes?" The sound was little more than a croak. But Angelo understood. It meant yes to so much more. Even to that which she most feared.

The instant his lips brushed hers Gemma knew her life would never be the same again. Every preconception she had of what it might've been like to be kissed by him vanished.

It was fire and light. Energy and emotion. Then his tongue touched hers and sparks shot through her. Adrenaline. And something magical.

She held her breath, didn't move in case the magic vanished. Then his tongue swept her mouth and the fire leapt inside her. Gemma groaned, closed her eyes and abandoned herself to the wonder.

When his fingers stroked the naked skin of her shoulder, every nerve ending went crazy. Frissons rippled down her spine and a reckless want followed. She moved closer, pressing herself up against him, until she felt the unmistakable ridge of his erection through the soft silk of her dress. It was a shock…a sign of how out of control this had become…but it was also incredibly satisfying.

Whatever the past held, Angelo wanted her. Now.

She sighed into his mouth, he deepened the kiss and

his breathing grew ragged. His hand closed on her shoulder and he pulled her against him.

At last he raised his head. "Do you remember that?"

Gemma stared at him, then regretfully shook her head.

He put her away from him, his hands shaking a little. "*Thiavlo*. I think we both need to cool down. Let's visit the casino—you always enjoyed that."

"Okay," she managed as he led her out from behind the inscrutable Hephaestus. Her knees shook. She had never felt less like gambling in her life.

Large double doors opened into the Apollo Club, the casino reserved for A-list clientele. Crystal chandeliers hung from the domed ceiling painted with beasts and heroes from myths Gemma knew well. The ambience in the room warned her that the stakes would be frighteningly high.

Angelo led her to a table with a group of men in tuxedos and two women—a blonde and a brunette—in evening gowns, jewels glittering at their necks and wrists. No voices hummed in here. Only the clatter of chips broke the solemn silence.

Murmuring an order, Angelo placed a wad of notes on the table. An elegant croupier in a long black dress slid several stacks of chips across the baize. Angelo passed the stacks to her, and Gemma realised he'd spent a small fortune for her to fritter away. She started to feel ill. "I can't gamble that kind of money."

The look he gave her was more than a little pointed. "It never troubled you in the past."

Gemma bit her lip. "What if I lose it all?"

Angelo shrugged. "Then I'll buy more."

And what would he expect from her then? Sex? Obviously that had happened in the past. Something within her shrivelled at the thought.

"No!" She shoved the chips back at him. "I might have forgotten how to do this, forgotten the rules."

"Try and we'll see."

"Angelo, I don't want to do this."

His gaze held hers. After a long moment he said, "All right. We'll see if we can penetrate that memory another way. Keep these—" he separated a small heap of chips "—in case you decide you want to play later."

She shook her head and pushed the chips away. "I don't feel like gambling tonight."

"Would you like to go for a drink?"

She nodded. This close she could see the laugh lines around his eyes, the glitter in his compelling eyes. He stilled in the act of gathering the chips and stared down at her.

"Gemma?"

With a start, she looked away, breaking the tenuous thread that linked them, and turned her head, searching for the source of the call that cut through the hush of the huge room.

"I *thought* it was you." The guy coming towards her was darkly tanned with Gallic features and carefully styled shaggy black hair. Gemma stared at him blankly.

The blonde at their table squealed in delight and grabbed his arm. He bent to kiss her cheek. Her much older companion didn't look happy.

The hand cupping Gemma's elbow tensed. "Did you invite him?" Angelo murmured in her ear.

"Invite him?" She swung around to cast Angelo a frown. "What are you talking about? I don't even know—" She broke off.

"Who he is," Angelo finished smoothly, and started to laugh, but Gemma noticed his eyes were devoid of humour. "I don't think Jean-Paul will appreciate being forgotten so soon."

"Who is he?" Gemma hissed.

"Jean-Paul Moreau." From Angelo's air of expectancy Gemma suspected the name was supposed to mean something to her. It didn't.

She lifted her shoulders and let them drop. "So…" she prompted.

"Your lover." Some ugly emotion flashed over Angelo's face then his features turned wooden. "The man I threw naked out of my—our—bed three years ago."

Three

Gemma stared.

Angelo's shocking revelation was the last thing she'd expected. Yet, judging by his narrow-eyed expression, he clearly believed it to be true.

She tested the discovery against her own belief. No, she couldn't accept it. Angelo must've made some awful mistake.

But before she could question him further, a mist of designer aftershave surrounded her. Then came a whisper of "*Cherie,* you are more beautiful than ever," and male lips nudged her cheek.

"Hello—" she tried frantically to remember his name "—Jean-Paul."

"I thought you were ignoring me, *cherie.* You stared straight through me earlier. I'm glad to know you remember your old friends."

Beside her Angelo snorted. Gemma shot him a warning look. She didn't want Jean-Paul knowing about the amnesia.

At least not yet.

Coming face-to-face with a man Angelo considered her lover had taken her aback. Much as she disliked Angelo, he had no reason to lie to her about the past. She needed to learn more.

With an extravagant flourish Jean-Paul produced a roll of euro notes from inside his jacket and signalled to the croupier. When the chips came, he slipped one pile across to Gemma. "For you, *cherie.*"

The smile Jean-Paul gave her was disconcertingly intimate. The secretive smile of a man to a woman he knew very, very well.

Gemma could sense Angelo's silent tension. Her stomach rolled over. "Thanks," she said stiltedly. Realising that she sounded terse she pointed to the unused chips on the table that Angelo had been in the process of gathering up before Jean-Paul's arrival. "But I have enough—and we're going for a drink."

Jean-Paul's gaze swept over her, explicit, knowing. Leaning towards her, he whispered, "*Cherie,* you're not the kind of woman ever to have enough. Here—" he slid a handful of chips towards her "—have a bet on me."

"Enough!" Angelo said harshly. A tanned arm hooked around Gemma's waist from behind, his other hand pushed his chips towards the croupier. "The lady doesn't want your chips." Against the length of her spine Gemma could feel Angelo's body through the thin silk of her dress. It was at once comforting and vaguely threatening. His arm lay coiled around her, under her breasts like a hard band, and awareness of his strength, his power, shivered through her.

It was the sudden ratcheting tension in his body that made her realise that Jean-Paul had moved. Within Angelo's hold, she twisted around on her stool. The two men faced each other like duelling adversaries.

Jean-Paul's gaze shifted from Angelo to Gemma and his mouth twisted. "It's like that, is it? *Cherie*, don't be fooled. Apollonides is the same man as three years ago. Work will always be his first mistress. Will that be enough for you this time around? Or will you come searching for warm arms, words of lo—"

"I said *enough*." Even Jean-Paul heard the suppressed violence in the whip-crack sound and took a hasty step back. "You go too far, Moreau. If I catch you near Gemma I will have you thrown off the island. Do you understand?"

A Gallic shrug and Jean-Paul smiled. "Keep cool, man. It doesn't mean a thing—it never did." But there was a wariness in his dark eyes that hadn't been there seconds before.

The last thing Gemma wanted was a scene. Already they were attracting the glances of people alerted by the bristling men and hissed words. The two women at their table were staring openly, while the croupier called for bets with a touch of desperation.

"Angelo—"

The arm tightened, cutting off her protest. "Gemma, you will not encourage this man. Moreau, you will keep your distance from Gemma. I've told you both before, I don't share my woman. Understand that." Releasing his hold on her, Angelo moved between her and Jean-Paul and with a hard glance at her, he added, "Both of you."

Then, in a swift movement, he swept the euro notes off the table and nodded at the croupier. "Come, Gemma. Let's go."

Without a glance in Jean-Paul's direction, Gemma slid from the stool.

The hand that came down on her shoulder was possessive, a warning. *His woman.* Angelo had warned Jean-Paul—and her—that he had no intention of sharing his woman, clearly not for the first time. Did that mean he still considered her his woman?

A frisson of dark emotion speared her. Gemma wasn't sure what to make of his claim and kept silent as they left the gaming room.

By the time they exited the elevator a floor down and walked out the hotel into the starry night, the anger inside Angelo was still simmering. Maintaining a terse silence, he strode along the path lit by decorative Victorian-style lamps. He was aware of the anxious glances Gemma kept casting him as she hurried along beside him, her high heels clicking against the terra-cotta flagstones.

"I'm sorry about what happened."

He shrugged. "It had to happen sooner or later. And it's only a matter of time before it happens again…before another man rises from the ashes of your past."

"I don't remember him," she said quickly.

Too quickly? "Meaning, you won't remember the others, either?" He shot her a derisive smile. "Poor bastard. I can almost feel pity for him."

Yet he had to admit he found it immensely satisfying that she didn't remember the Frenchman. Especially after…

Hell!

"I knew about Jean-Paul, saw you both in my bed with my own eyes." His tone took on a dark edge. "I can give you details of how you were straddling him, your knees around his hips, your bare breasts bouncing and the satin sheets—*my* satin sheets—crumpled around you. Your skin like a pearl against—"

"Stop." Gemma came to a jarring halt. "I don't want to hear this." Her head bent, she stared at the shadowy footpath and tension hunched her bare shoulders. She shivered as a sharp gust of sea-wind cut through the night.

"If I tell you what I saw, what I can still see so clearly, it might help you remember." He knew his bitterness was showing. But he wanted to hurt her, cut to the heart of her. Humiliate her as he'd been humiliated. "How many more men like Jean-Paul will there be? Men that I don't know of? Men that you don't remember?"

Gemma shivered again.

Angered by her lack of response, he said, "Tell me, Gemma, how many more?"

"I don't know," she said in a very small voice.

"Look at me." His hands closed on her shoulders. Her skin was like ice. He swung her round and her eyes snapped open revealing her bewilderment as she stumbled on her high heels.

"Careful!" He tightened his grip and couldn't help noticing how soft her skin felt.

She ducked away. Her heel gave and she almost fell.

With an exasperated imprecation he yanked her upright. "Are you okay?"

"No thanks to you." She wrenched herself free. "If

you hadn't grabbed me like some Neanderthal I'd have been fine."

"Neanderthal?" He didn't know whether to laugh or to swear at the crack. *"Neanderthal?"*

Gemma's heart sank as she absorbed his outrage. Then she stiffened as her own indignation kicked in. It *was* his doing that she'd nearly fallen. He'd spun her round. Ever since Jean-Paul's arrival he'd been acting like a jealous jerk. She didn't have to put up with it.

Tossing back her hair, she lifted her chin. "Yes. Neanderthal. You know—some primitive three-hundred pound gorilla type." Her heart was galloping as she stared at him defiantly, waiting for his response.

For a moment he simply stood there. Then he gurgled something that sounded like *gorilla* and his arms shot out.

She gave a squeak. And then it was too late.

He had her in a hard hold, his fingers imprinted on her shoulders, and his lips slanted across hers, grinding down against the softness cooled by the night breeze. She wriggled and murmured a protest.

He raised his head, and she gulped a much-needed breath. "So I'm a gorilla, am I?"

Hastily she shook her head. A mad urge to laugh bubbled through Gemma. Then his mouth was back, open and hungry on hers, and all coherent thought left her. His tongue stroked the soft, tender skin inside her cheeks. Heat sliced through her, a restless yearning started to build. The desire he'd ignited when he'd kissed her in the alcove returned in full force. Gemma's head spun. What the hell was happening to her?

His arms tightened, drawing her up against him. He was already aroused.

The realisation sent a wave of reckless euphoria coursing through her. Her bones softened, and in her lower body the heat started to spread. Her hips seemed to have developed a life of their own and moved in slow circles against him. Angelo groaned.

His hot breath rushed into her mouth and the intimacy turned her knees to liquid. Gemma staggered backward, her heels digging into the turf, and Angelo followed, his thighs moving against hers in an erotic dance, their mouths devouring each other.

The roughness of a tree trunk stopped Gemma backing up. Angelo didn't pause until he had her plastered against the trunk, his body reamed up against hers in the dark space under the wide canopy of branches, his hands twisted in the tangled mass of her hair. Her nipples pebbled, aching under the press of his body. Here, in the silent darkness, the golden glow of the lamplight seemed far away.

The pressure on her mouth gave a little and then the tip of his tongue started to outline her lips, slowly, deliberately, his hands holding her head, positioning her for maximum impact.

It was teasing, frustrating. She wanted him to kiss her. Intimately. *"More."* The demand was torn from her. She butted her hips forward, finding the length of his erection and started to rock back and forth. She wanted more of his mouth, more of his touch…more… of the intense want ripping through her.

But he kept the tongue strokes light and toying and she writhed against him.

When Angelo finally lifted his head, Gemma moaned a protest. In the stillness of the night the sound of their breathing was hoarse and ragged. His fingers fiddled at her nape and a moment later she felt the straps of her halter dress and the bra beneath give.

A warm hand slipped under the fabric and stroked the bare flesh of her breast. His fingers brushed the nub; sensation shot through her and she gasped, arching against the tree. He repeated the motion. She tensed as a rush of heat pooled beneath her panties.

"Ghhh." The sound that escaped her was foreign, incomprehensible even to her own ears. Rising on tiptoe, Gemma rocked harder, rubbing herself against his solid flesh, concentrating on that sensitive part of her—the part that touched him, aroused him, despite the rasp of the fabric that separated them. Then his leg moved, bracing his weight, so that the hardness in the front of his trousers fitted in the space between her legs.

Her eyes tightly closed, her head flung back, Gemma focused on the fingertips massaging her nipple, on the sensation spreading out hotter and hotter from the junction between her legs.

She started to pant and the desperate heat climbed higher…higher…within her. She rocked faster still, rubbing against him, and he responded, his hips moving back and forth, the friction building—building until Gemma knew that she was poised on the lip of the void.

The taunting, teasing touch on her nipples tightened. And when his tongue entered her mouth in wild, consuming thrusts a bolt of electric sensation shot through Gemma.

Turned on beyond belief, Gemma gasped, a wild, keening sound. Her body tightened, the sensitive point at the apex of her legs caught fire and the convulsions began.

She sagged against the tree, spent and dizzy, her pulse pumping furiously through her head. Her legs had turned to water, and she suspected that had the tree not supported her she would've collapsed.

Angelo lifted his head and withdrew his hand from her breast. Her body cooled as he stepped away, his expression unfathomable in the criss-cross shadows of the branches.

"Maybe that will help you remember!"

God, how she hated him. At his awful words she fumbled for the straps behind her neck, but her fingers were shaking so much she couldn't tie them. Finally, with an impatient mutter Angelo stepped forward. But this time he kept his body from touching hers, and unexpectedly Gemma ached for the loss. The pull of the straps tightening as he knotted them was unbearably intimate and Gemma searched desperately for something to say to break the ghastly, growing silence.

What was there to say to the man who'd pleasured her so thoroughly without taking the time to remove her dress or her panties? Hell, despite her dislike and distrust, she'd let him do what he wanted, touch where he wanted without a murmur.

She shuddered with shame.

Telling herself she despised him didn't help. She'd driven him on, rubbing herself against him like… Oh, God! She flushed at the memory of what she'd done… her lack of restraint. Fully clad, Angelo had touched her with only with his mouth and the fingertips of one hand and brought her more ecstasy than she could ever remember experiencing.

She wanted to run. To hide. Before her composure gave way.

"I'll find my way from here. You don't have to come any farther." Then she closed her eyes as she replayed her own words and waited for him to point out that he hadn't come. Yet.

"I will walk you to your unit." His voice was colder than winter. "The sooner your contract ends and you leave Strathmos, the better for both of us."

"I'll leave tomorrow," Gemma blurted out, her eyes stinging. "Leave me alone. I don't want your company."

Once inside her unit, Gemma flipped the kettle on with hands that trembled, and blinked away the tears that blurred her vision. Feeling utterly wretched, she craved a mug of camomile tea to soothe her shattered nerves while the aftershocks of their terrifyingly passionate encounter quaked through her.

She couldn't stay.

She would leave Strathmos tomorrow, catch the first ferry out—even if it meant breaking her contract and putting her professional reputation on the line. She could not do this.

Never had it crossed her mind that she would melt under Angelo Apollonides's touch, press her body up against his, encourage his kisses. He was a suave playboy. No one knew better than she.

Oh, God. How had she gotten herself into this fix? Distraught, Gemma speared her shaky fingers through her hair.

She needed to get a grip. Fighting for control, she tried to think analytically about what had happened out there, under the cold stars. Okay, so she'd provoked him. Intentionally. But she hadn't expected him to react so fiercely, to move so quickly. His cool eyes, his mocking smile, his legion of beautiful cookie-cutter lovers had indicated Angelo wasn't a man given to impulse. That devastating kiss—and what had followed—stunned her.

He was far more dangerous than she'd ever known.

When the kettle clicked off, she reached into the cupboard for a mug and poured boiling water over the teabag. *Why had she risked all the ground she'd made by provoking him?* What had she hoped to gain? What was it about Angelo that made her itch to disconcert him? To prove to him she wasn't the woman he thought he was?

Cradling the mug between her hands, she propped her elbows on the bench top. The photo at the end of the bench top mocked her.

Setting her tea down, she picked up the photo. It looked like such an idyllic family. Mum and Dad flanking their smiling, all-grown-up daughter against a backdrop of lovingly tended rosebushes. Tears pricked again. Gemma craved a dose of her mother's kind common sense. Checking her watch she calculated that in New Zealand it would be morning. She picked up the handset from the wall and punched in the familiar number of her childhood home.

"Hello?"

Despite the distance her mother's voice was clear and familiar.

Gemma swallowed the lump in her throat. "It's me, Mum."

"Sweetheart, I'm so glad you've called. I've been worried sick about you!"

"I should've called sooner." Gemma had known her parents were worried. She'd been avoiding their concern. "But you know I had to come."

"Yes." Her mother's voice held a touch of resignation. "Has it helped?"

The grief counsellor had supported Gemma's determination in the face of her parents' objections. Closure came in strange ways. And that's what this trip was about, closure. "I don't know. Mum, I'm so confused." Gemma thought of Angelo's effect on her, how he only had to touch her to send her up in flames and gulped. "Sometimes I feel like I'm losing my mind." But tomorrow that would end. She would leave…and never see Angelo Apollonides again. It was for the best— even if it meant she'd never know the truth…

"How is Dad?"

"Fine."

"No, I mean, how is he handling my coming to Strathmos? He was very upset when I left."

Her mother sighed. "He's worried. And it's opened up the memories about your sister's death. He's afraid of what might happen to you."

"Tell him I'm fine…and I love him."

"He's gone back to therapy. The doctor says he's over the worst of the depression. For him, like you, the hardest part was not knowing why Mandy died."

"Double trouble, that's what Dad used to call us." Staring at the photo, Gemma searched the face of her twin for answers. Mandy had died, unhappy and lost. But no one knew why. Only Angelo could provide the answers that would let her father—and Gemma herself—find a little peace.

Closure.

That's what they all needed.

And that was why she could not tell Angelo to go to hell and walk away. Cold seeped in, chilling her all the way to her soul.

She could not leave tomorrow.

"Oh, *sweetheart.* Come home."

"I can't." Her lips barely moved. "I have to find out what happened to Mandy. For all our sakes. Then we can get on with our lives."

"Oh, Gemma. Your sister wouldn't want you to suffer like this, she'd want you to remember the special times you had together."

"I know. But I need to understand what happened to her…what this bastard did to her and why she reacted like she did. Dad and you need to know, too."

"Your father and I don't want you meddling with this man." Her mother's voice was anxious. "He's wealthy, powerful. He could hurt you."

Like he hurt Mandy.

Gemma knew what her mother was thinking. But the words remained unspoken.

"Mum…" Gemma's voice trailed away. She thought of what had just happened between her and Angelo. If her parents knew about that…they'd be on the next flight out to rescue her.

"Have you spoken to him? What did he say?"

Reluctant to admit that she hadn't confronted Angelo about Mandy's death, and even more loath for her mother to discover that Angelo believed she was Mandy, Gemma spoke in a rush. "I wanted to find out what kind of man he is first."

"And what kind of man is he?"

Compelling. Passionate. "It's difficult to explain."

"Gemma, be careful." The sigh came over the miles. "You're not Mandy. Chasing after trouble was her speciality, not yours. You were always the sensible one, Gemma."

Her mother was right, Mandy had always been a little…wild. Taking Gemma's passport and credit card to Strathmos and assuming Gemma's identity was only one of the pranks Mandy had played.

Oh, Mandy, what happened on Strathmos?

Gemma couldn't help thinking about the familiarity in the Frenchman's tone earlier, his easy kiss. She remembered Angelo's hard gaze, the coiled tension in his muscled body. She remembered the taste of his mouth—hot and seductive against hers—the thrill of his body pressing into hers and her pleasure as she came apart under his touch.

Once again confusion and turmoil wrestled within her. God! How could she teach the bastard the lesson he deserved if she desired him?

And how could she face him again?

Gemma squeezed her eyes shut. How on earth could she have reacted like that to the man who had destroyed her sister?

Four

Gemma tossed and turned for most of the night. Several times she jerked awake from confusing dreams of what had happened in her sister's life. Beneath it all festered an uneasiness about the disturbing passion that had flared between herself and Angelo. Just before dawn the pitter-patter of rain against the window pane lulled her into a restless sleep.

In the morning she clambered out of bed, crossed to the window and hitched the curtain back. No sun peeked through the cloud cover. The trees outside swayed in the wind. But at least the rain had subsided. With her morning free of rehearsals and her next show scheduled for later that evening, Gemma decided to make for the beach to go windsurfing. That was one place where wet and wind wouldn't matter. And it would certainly shake the dark mood that gripped her and take her mind off Mandy, Jean-Paul and... Angelo.

Pulling on a sleek black maillot, she called reception to check that no storms were forecasted, then grabbed her wet suit out of the cupboard and trod into a pair of ancient sneakers. A couple of bananas, a bottle of water and a towel, and she was ready to go.

The beach was deserted. To Gemma's relief, there were no whitecaps on the water. A gust of wind tugged at her hair as she hauled a windsurfing board out of the stack. Dragging the board into the sea, she waded calf-deep into the water and waited with both hands on the boom. When a puff of wind came, she pushed the mast straight up and stepped onto the centre of the board. Shifting her feet, Gemma adjusted the sail and, looking upwind, she turned the board to the open sea.

The sail filled and she took off, the wind rushing past her ears. She barely noticed the rain and her worries evaporated as she raced across the water.

She welcomed the freedom.

A couple of hours later Gemma became aware of another windsurfer on the water, coming towards her through the rain. Leaning her mast back, the nose of her board started to turn upwind across the face of the wind, away from the intruder. But the other windsurfer gained on her, trespassing on her solitude.

A quick glance at her watch showed that she still had lots of time before her show. It wasn't often that she had the sea to herself. Why would she go in simply because someone was crowding her? There was a whole sea for the two of them. If she tacked away, perhaps the other windsurfer would get the hint.

But the larger black-and-white sail continued to bear down on her. Glaring at him—it was undoubtedly a male figure—Gemma's annoyance grew when she recognised the windsurfer.

Angelo.

Setting a course upwind, Gemma decided to force him to yield to her. A glint of white as his teeth flashed. *He knew what she was up to.*

Determined to get ahead, she started to work every ounce of speed out of her rig. The board responded willingly and elation swept through her.

Then she saw that Angelo had taken up her challenge.

For a moment she thought that they might collide. She faltered, her board wobbled and her nerve almost gave in, before he gave way, falling back to sail in her wake. Her sail shivering under the pressure of the wind, she skimmed across the water, while her heart beat rapidly at the near miss—and the euphoria that came from racing the wind…and besting Angelo.

Angelo stared after Gemma not sure whether to whistle in admiration or holler at her recklessness. She was going full tilt, not giving an inch. He pointed his board to a destination upwind of where she was headed, and he set off after her.

The breeze blew on his face, lighter on the inside near the shore. He came down the line he'd planned, unfazed by the rain, tacking with speed and closing his distance on Gemma.

She turned, glancing over her shoulder as he gained on her. He could see the determination in her stance. This was no beginner. She was going to give him a good run.

They battled it out downwind. Her jaw was set. She wasn't giving an inch. She wanted to win. Despite the rain, her hair streamed behind her like a bright banner, a lithe graceful figure in tune with the elements.

Never had he wanted her as much as he did at the moment. She looked elemental and a little elusive. Not the sure thing he'd always considered her.

Working furiously, Angelo finally notched ahead and threw a triumphant smile over his shoulder, confident that the race was done.

The next instant the wind dropped and the rain eased. Both boards slowed. Angelo bit back a curse at being deprived of a clear victory. He dropped down to straddle the board and, glancing sideways, saw that Gemma had dropped onto her stomach and was already paddling with her arms and making for the shore.

Pacing himself, he kept abreast of her, his powerful arms stroking through the water. But she didn't look at him, she kept her gaze firmly ahead.

In the shallows, keeping her face averted, Gemma leapt off the board, dragging it in behind her, intensely conscious of Angelo following close behind.

Flutters of apprehension started deep in her stomach, and the battle of the last half hour between them was forgotten as the memory of what had happened between them last night rose in her mind.

She didn't know how she was going to face him.

The attendant, now at his post, came running to take the board. She gave a brief, abstracted smile of thanks. Her saturated sneakers squishing with water, she hurried to where she'd dropped her towel and water bottle earlier. Collapsing onto a damp wooden bench, she uncapped the bottle and took a long sip, her heart banging against her ribs as Angelo approached.

He stopped beside her. She stilled, then took another sip, pretending to ignore him, while every nerve ending quivered warily at his closeness.

"You never told me you could windsurf."

The rasp of the zip sounded loud in the silence. Gemma was achingly aware of his peeling off his wet suit and slinging it over the back of the bench. Underneath he wore a pair of boardshorts that rode low on his hips. The unwelcome memory of last night clear in her mind, Gemma tried not to notice that his stomach was taut and tanned, the defined muscles revealing that he worked out regularly—or led a very active lifestyle.

Gemma whipped her gaze away and shrugged. "I don't know why I didn't tell you. I would've thought I had." Why had Mandy not told him? Especially as it was clear it was something Angelo excelled at. Her parents had paid for lessons for both her and Mandy to learn to windsurf down at Buckland's Beach, near their childhood home. Mandy had been more interested in flirting with the youths in the class than learning to sail. Deciding to distract him with flattery Gemma added, "You're good. Those were some great moves out there."

But Angelo didn't bite. "So, when are you leaving?"

Gemma drew a deep, shuddering breath. "I'm not." His expression never altered, but she sensed his sudden tension.

"Last night you said you were going, why have you changed your mind?"

Even though his tone remained even, his eyes told a different story. Her gaze fell before his challenging stare, landing on his legs. His thighs were solid, the skin darkened to a deep bronze by the Greek sun. She felt herself flush and quickly looked away over the sea. She didn't want this awful awareness of this man. "Because my reputation would be mud in entertainment circles if I walked away from my contract."

"I would see to it that didn't happen."

He wanted her gone that much? Gemma swallowed, then said baldly, "I can't go, I need the money."

A coolness entered his voice. "Is this where I'm supposed to offer to pay you to leave?"

"No!" Gemma jerked her head up to stare at him, horrified by the conclusion he'd drawn. "But I've got a contract and I'm entitled to payment for doing my job. I need it."

"What do you need the money for?" Angelo dropped down beside her and his arm stretched along the back of the bench, so that it rested behind her head.

She thought furiously. "Medical expenses," she said at last, trying to ignore his arm. It wasn't easy. "From the…er…car accident." She swallowed again and stared out over the sea.

"That's what caused your amnesia?"

Damn. What to say now?

The silence stretched. He was waiting for her reply. Gemma discovered she wasn't crazy about lying to him. Strange, because she'd never thought it would worry her in the least. Not after what he'd done.

"Witnesses say it was a hit and run," she expanded, sticking to the story she'd originally planned. "Luckily when I came round in hospital I remembered who I was. But I don't remember anything about you, about Strathmos…or anything that happened for a while after I left Strathmos."

"So you're suffering from retrograde amnesia. You lost the events immediately before the accident."

Retrograde amnesia? Gemma blinked. "Uh…yes." His interest took her aback. She gave him a weak smile. "Have you been doing research?"

"A little. Did you experience any memory loss after the accident?"

This time she was prepared. "Yes. There was some anterograde amnesia. I remember waking up in hospital. I don't remember the accident itself—or getting to the hospital. The specialists did say that the events I could no longer recall before the accident might return as time passed. But to date they haven't. I lost several weeks of my life." She delivered the explanation as she'd prepared it.

"Was there any other damage?" His fingers brushed her shoulder. Despite the thick protection of the Neoprene wet suit, Gemma felt as though she'd been scorched.

"No, I was fortunate," she said a trifle huskily as shivers coursed through her.

"Nothing lucky about it," he said abruptly. "Such an accident should never have happened. Did the police catch the perpetrator?"

"No." Gemma fidgeted. She hadn't expected his concern and outrage on her behalf. She folded her arms across her stomach, feeling terrible. Then she recalled her father's depression, her mother's tears after Mandy's unnecessary death. Instantly her heart hardened. "Now can you understand why I need money?"

"What will you do when you finish here?"

"My agent is looking for something for me." There had been offers, but Gemma hadn't been in a hurry to take another booking. She hadn't been sure how long she needed on Strathmos to learn the truth.

"So long as you know that your contract to sing here will not be extended. I don't want you here."

Gemma gulped. That was pretty direct. It also meant that she had less than three weeks to find out the truth. "I understand."

Two days passed without catching sight of Angelo. On Wednesday morning Gemma lounged beside the resort's heated outdoor pool, soaking up the mild early morning sunshine. She'd heard that Angelo sometimes swam laps after breakfast before the resort guests started to congregate.

Huge sheets of glass shut out the unpredictable autumn wind without obscuring the view of the Aegean. In the centre of the pool a marble quartet of golden winged horses danced under the spray that jetted from three tall fountains. Through half-closed eyes, Gemma could almost imagine the mythical beasts thundering across the heavens, steered by the sun god.

A young poolside waiter had just delivered a tall glass topped with a pink umbrella and a row of cherries on a swizzle stick when a familiar voice shattered the fantasy.

"So this is where you've been hiding."

Tensing, Gemma wished she was wearing more than

the tiny bikini with the skimpy bandana top. Hidden behind sunglasses, she said, "Don't you have more important things to do than look for me?"

Angelo waved his hand dismissively. "You told me you are here for the money. Right?"

"Y-es," she stretched the word out, waiting, wondering why his eyes had turned as hard as stone.

He dropped down on the lounger beside hers; only a low glass-topped table on which her drink stood separated them. Uncomfortably conscious of his closeness, Gemma pushed her sunglasses firmly up her nose, grateful for the protection they offered from his icy scrutiny.

"I've just learned you wanted this contract badly enough to take a drop in pay." His voice was edged in steel. "I want to know why. How could you afford to do that with the medical expenses you cried about only a couple of days ago?"

Raising her shoulder, Gemma dropped it with false aplomb. "I took the drop because I was desperate for money. I needed an income—I haven't been getting regular work."

His gaze glittered with suspicion. "You once told me that one of the joys of being an exotic dancer is that there's always work. So if you were short of work why sing? Why not dance?"

Gemma forced herself not to shudder. She'd never understood why Mandy danced or how she put up with the hoards of leering men—even if the money was good. "Uh—I don't do that anymore. I love singing." That, at least, was true. "And singing pays more when I get the right spots, which I'm getting more often. I'm on the rise."

"What's this?"

Something in his sharp tone turned her head. He was scowling at the glass the waiter had brought. She frowned, puzzled at his ferocity.

"You can't drink before you sing."

"Not even fruit juice?" she asked tartly. He looked unconvinced, so Gemma picked the glass up and thrust it at him. "Here, sniff it."

"Very clever." At her baffled frown, he added. "Given that your preferred drink is vodka, sniffing won't help much. Not with the overpowering flavour of pineapple."

Of course! Mandy had always been partial to vodka. "My only vice," Gemma said at last.

"*Only* vice?" His smile was sharklike. Setting the glass down, he leaned closer.

This close up his eyes were mesmerizing. The vibrant turquoise irises were surrounded by a row of lashes too long for a man. Dark brows arched over the top. No question about it, Angelo Apollonides was the most gorgeous male she had ever set eyes on. Pity he was not her type.

"It's the only one I can think of right now," she said carelessly. "If I thought about it very hard, I might discover one or two more."

His mouth flattened. "Try. I'm sure you will find there are more vices that you will remember. Like lying."

Gemma's breath left her in a rush.

"When did I lie?" Did he know? She gave him a searching look as adrenaline started to pump through her. *God.* What would he do if he discovered—

"When I discovered you'd taken a drop in pay, I thought you lied to me. That you had another agenda. Don't ever lie to me."

She almost collapsed from relief. So she glared at him. "I'm *not* lying. I do need money. My credit card is a little over-extended." The thirty-thousand dollar debt merited a bigger description than *little*.

"Too much shopping and partying?"

If he only knew. While Mandy had been a party animal, Gemma preferred spending her spare time outdoors. Walking. Windsurfing. Or simply attending concerts in parks. Simple pleasures, not the sophisticated pursuits his mistresses would enjoy.

She pursed her lips. How could she admit how much money had vanished, and that she had no idea where it had gone? The large cash withdrawals her credit-card statements reflected told her nothing.

"You had no debt three years ago. And some nice pieces of jewellery." He gave a pointed stare at the ring she wore. The ring Mandy had given her just before she had died and Angelo had claimed to have bought for Mandy in Monaco.

"I don't know what happened to all that," she said honestly.

He gave her a searching look. "You don't remember?"

She nodded.

"I was more than generous," he said. "I indulged your desire to party, to shop until your cupboards were overflowing. If you'd behaved better, you might not be in this predicament."

Surely Angelo wasn't suggesting they might still be together? Not when she knew the kind of man he was. A playboy. A man who traded one beautiful woman for another, as soon as their temporary sell-by date was over.

Her lip curled. "You mean, if I was still your mistress? Putting up with your demands, your—"

"I thought you'd forgotten everything. So how do you remember how demanding I was?" His tone held a sensual rasp, belied by his shrewd gaze.

"I read gossip cuttings. How do you think I learned about our affair?"

He reached out and put finger a finger under her chin. He put enough pressure to tilt her head up, so that he could stare down into her eyes. "So you came here not only to earn money and regain your memory, but to learn more about us?"

The sudden flare of heat that followed in the wake of the touch of that one finger shocked her. *No.* She was not going to respond to his very obvious attraction. He was the last man on earth to whom she could afford to be attracted.

A spoilt playboy who'd had a fortune handed to him on a plate. A dilettante who destroyed people without compunction. Keeping her voice level she said, "I know exactly what kind of man you are."

"Do you really?" He raised a dark eyebrow, looming over her.

Too close. Too male. Too…everything.

She backpedaled. "I don't remember anything, but I know how you make me feel."

"And how is that?" The pressure of the pad of his index finger lessened. The tip trailed down her throat and settled just below the tender hollow at the base of her neck. The touch felt like a brand.

Oh, no. She spotted the trap too late. She swallowed. "Repelled."

He bared his teeth in triumph at the tiny give away as her throat moved. "Ah, you tempt me to prove you a liar."

Gemma gave an uneasy laugh. "Perhaps I haven't been completely honest with you."

His pupils expanded. "Go on."

"I came here to ask for your help." She sucked in a breath. "I woke alone in a hospital in London with no memory of how I got there, who I'd been with at the time of the accident or where I'd been."

His hand dropped away.

Gemma could breathe again.

Until he spoke. "You weren't able to track down information from the people with you at the time of the accident?"

She had to be careful. She couldn't afford to trip herself up. "The only clue about where I'd been was a bunch of old pay slips from Palace of Poseidon." She'd found them in her sister's things. "Later I found out that I'd worked here…that we'd had an affair."

More lies. It hadn't been later. Mandy had e-mailed her from Strathmos, crowing about the fabulously wealthy man she'd landed.

Gemma stared at him defiantly. "That's why I'm here. I thought if I came…back…met you, I might re-member something about—" she paused "—my past."

His expression altered subtly. He came closer. "Is it working?"

"No." Her voice turned husky. She picked up a towel and draped it over her bare, exposed tummy. "I had hoped by staying on Strathmos some things might come back to me. But they haven't." She paused for a beat, peered up at him over the top of her sunglasses. "But perhaps if you helped, if you let me ask you some questions, maybe something you say might act as a trigger. And the past might come back to me."

She waited, holding her breath, her blood hammering in her head, causing it to ache with tension. What had Angelo done to reduce Mandy from a confident, somewhat reckless party girl to a pale, shaking ghost of her former self?

She *had* to find out.

At last he gave a curt nod. "But if it doesn't work, that's it. Okay? You leave as soon as your contract is complete." He rose to his feet. "We'll start tonight, after your show."

"I'd rather meet in the mornings."

"I'm a busy man. If you want my help then you'll have to meet me tonight. In my suite."

"No." Gemma shook her head emphatically, her hair swirling around her face. The last thing she wanted was to be alone with him. The attraction he held terrified her. While she desperately wanted to know what he'd done to her twin, she was not about to let him destroy her in the process. "I'll meet you after the show in the Dionysus bar."

For a moment Gemma thought she'd lost him. Then he said, "You're on."

Five

When Gemma hurried into the Dionysus bar later that night it was buzzing. She hesitated, scanning the press of people, until Angelo rose from a table near the window. Outside, the resort's landscaped gardens were lit by floodlights. Beyond them she could see the lights of vessels winking out on the dark sea.

"Sorry I'm late," she gasped. "I had to shower and change." She indicated to the shimmery wraparound dress that she'd slipped on.

"No problem." He pulled out a chair for her. "How did the performance go?"

"Good. It never fails to put me on a high."

Angelo beckoned to a waiter. "What can I order for you to drink?"

"A white-wine cooler would be good—with lots of sparkling water, ice and a little lime, please."

He gave her a long look. "Are you sure that's what you want? Your performance is over. You can have something more…robust if you want."

The euphoria left her. She sagged into the chair. "I don't drink much of the hard stuff. But thanks."

Gemma watched him as he spoke to the waiter. What had his relationship with her sister been like? Mandy had always loved to party…and the kind of men she'd picked tended to have no problem with that. But Angelo seemed almost disapproving. Not what she'd expected from his playboy persona at all.

When he turned back, Gemma—unable to let his comment pass—said, "Strange for an hotelier to be watching his guests' liquor consumption." With a sweep of her arm, she encompassed the full-to-capacity bar. "Can't be good for business."

"You're not a guest, you're an employee," he said quellingly. "And you don't have a great track record."

"What do you mean?"

He shook his head. "Be grateful that you don't remember."

"But I *want* to know."

"You're better served moving on from those events. It's enough for you to know that you had a…problem."

A problem that he had exacerbated?

Gemma studied his expression. To be fair, it didn't look like he'd approved of Mandy's antics…whatever they had been. Was it possible that he'd had nothing to do with Mandy's slide from grace?

He forced me. I loved him. I wanted to please him. I was ready to do whatever he wanted. And it made me feel good. I'm so sorry for failing you all.

The memory of Mandy's words caused Gemma to steel herself. No. Angelo was *not* uninvolved. He'd destroyed her twin.

But before she could tell him what a low-life skunk she considered him, their drinks arrived.

Angelo passed a long glass to her. "So what do you want to ask me?"

She stared at him blankly.

"That's why we're here, remember?" His smiled was sardonic. "So that you can ask me questions, to try and jolt your memory."

Oh, yes. She gave herself a gentle shake. Nothing would be served by telling him what she thought of him. Better to focus on what she'd come here for—to learn what had happened to Mandy…to find a way to make Angelo pay.

Gemma took a sip of her drink. It was cool and refreshing. "You wanted to know why I need money. In addition to the medical expenses—" she broke off, reluctant to perpetuate that lie, then blurted out, "I want to know why there was thirty thousand owing on my credit card. Do you know where it went?"

"I have no idea."

"I drew cash out with my credit card and ran through it in your casinos, didn't I?" She was pushing him now, but she wanted answers. She wanted him to confess what he'd gotten Mandy into. "*Your* casinos. *Your* fault I'm thirty-thousand in the red."

"You liked to gamble…I didn't force you. But I wouldn't call you an addict."

Gemma flinched. "But it would've been more than I could afford."

"Your chips went on my account. It didn't cost you a euro. You must have accumulated your debts—" he picked the word with fastidious care "—after you left me."

"So where I did I go from Strathmos?"

He lifted a negligent shoulder. "I have no idea."

"Nor did you care—certainly not enough to buy me a ticket to make sure I reached home safely."

A frown creased his brow, he picked up his drink and leaned back. "I'm a generous man. I gave you a more than a plentiful allowance while you lived with me. Gold cards, a supply of cash that you ran through like water." There was distaste in his tone now. "You could have saved that for a rainy day."

Gemma opened her mouth to argue, then shut it again. His words held the unmistakeable ring of truth.

"I regret the hit-and-run left you floundering for your memory." The sympathy in his eyes faded as he continued, "But you're an adult. You've worked in nightclubs in London, Paris. You considered New Zealand a backwater. I assumed you'd simply find another big city, another big-spending benefactor to fund your love of the high life."

She blinked. While he'd clearly enjoyed having Mandy in his bed, it didn't sound like he'd held her twin in high regard. Poor Mandy.

He set his glass down. "After I found you with Moreau I didn't give a damn where you were going. Right then I hoped you'd drown in the sea. You'd betrayed me, in the worst way that a woman can betray a man. I couldn't wait to see the back of you."

Gemma flinched at his bitter words. Yet under the white-hot anger she suspected that Angelo was telling the truth. He *didn't* know where Mandy had gone after leaving him. Could that mean that she'd misjudged him? Had he had nothing to do with Mandy's problems? Had they only started after her sister left Strathmos?

Her shoulders sagged. She'd had such high hopes that Angelo would provide the key to the puzzle. Then she thought about what he'd said, and lifted her head. "Did I leave the island with Jean-Paul?"

He shrugged. "It's possible. I wanted him out my sight, too."

Perhaps the Frenchman could provide a clue to what had happened. Angelo's face had tightened at the mention of the other man. She changed the subject. "You said that you inherited a string of family hotels from your grandfather. How did they transform into this?" Gemma gestured to the bar and, beyond it, the resort.

"On my twenty-first birthday, I inherited three islands and a chain of three-star holiday hotels geared to foreign budget tourists. My grandfather had been ill for a while. The hotels were shabby, showing their age. While they were well booked over the summer months, they were deserted in winter. I knew I could do more. I wanted resorts where occupancy was guaranteed all year round."

"That's why you went for casinos?"

He nodded. "But I wanted more than glamorous casinos. I wanted places where everyone in the family would have a good time. That meant themed resorts, cinemas, a variety of shows that would draw people back again."

"You achieved everything you set out to do."

He nodded. "It took a while. I first worked at upgrading the hotels I had. I knew the first spectacular resort had to be built here at Strathmos. It was my dream. I hadn't been back to the island since I left as an eighteen-year-old. Once I got it up, Poseidon was born."

"And now Poseidon's resorts are associated with worlds of fantasy." She tried to hide her admiration by giving the words a bite. "The Golden Cavern. The Never-Ending River." She named some famous drawcards.

His gaze narrowed. "You remember? You remember visiting them with me?"

The damned amnesia. She'd nearly given herself away. Slowly she shook her head. "I told you, I tried to put together the missing parts of my memory so I read up about our relationship in the tabloids. There were bits about Poseidon's Resorts, too. Like their fantasy themes and what they're worth today. About how innovative you were." And on the Internet there had been endless details about the wealthy, powerful and good-looking Angelo Apollonides, Mr. Eligible Bachelor Billionaire of the Year. But she wasn't telling him any of that. The last thing she wanted was for him to think he interested her. Gemma shifted, uncomfortable with where this conversation was heading.

She could barely hide her relief when the duty manager arrived and whispered into Angelo's ear.

"I'm sorry," he apologised. "I am needed. And we've barely gotten started."

"Don't worry. We can talk again some other time."

"Shall I order you another drink?"

"No, I'm done." She pushed the empty glass aside. "I might wander over to one of the coffee bars. And then I'll make my way back to my room. I can use an early night. Don't worry about me."

He rose and gave her a slow smile. "I find that I can't help worrying about you." And her heart twisted.

And then he was gone.

Still thinking about that delicious smile—and her reaction to it—Gemma picked up her purse and threaded her way through the packed bar to the exit—where she almost ran into Jean-Paul.

"Steady, *cherie*." He caught her by the elbows. "Can I buy you a drink?" His dark eyes lingered on her appreciatively.

Sensitive to Angelo's accusation that Mandy had cheated on him with the Frenchman, and Angelo had warned her in no uncertain terms to stay away from him, Gemma's first response was to refuse. But what if Mandy had left Strathmos with Jean-Paul? Gemma hesitated, then thrust her scruples aside.

She needed to talk to this man.

"I'd love a drink." She gave him a bright smile to make up for her hesitation. He was back in minutes with two glasses.

"What is it?" she asked, eyeing the clear liquid uneasily.

"Surely you didn't think I could forget, *cherie?* You're the only woman I ever knew who drank triple vodka and tonic like water." He gave her a very knowing smile. "The secret of your success, you called it. And what made you so exciting."

Angelo strode out of the Apollo Club. It hadn't taken long to calm two furious patrons after an accusation of cheating in the discreet back room where a poker game with extremely high stakes was being played.

In the elevator he greeted an American IT billionaire and his wife who came to the Palace every few months.

Hurrying out the elevator, he glanced at his watch. Gemma should be back in her unit by now. Downstairs, he stopped beside a porter kiosk and called reception requesting to be put through to her room. It rang unanswered.

Perhaps she was still in one of the coffee shops.

He made his way to the entertainment complex. He didn't find her in the first coffee shop. Nor in large alcove with soft armchairs where a pianist played Chopin. But as he passed the Dionysus Bar he caught a glimpse of copper flame.

Gemma.

Frowning, he ground to a halt and looked again.

It *was* Gemma. And she was not alone. Jean-Paul Moreau was standing beside her barstool, his arm resting on the bar beside his drink, looking utterly enthralled by her.

What the hell was she doing with Moreau?

He'd warned her to keep away from the man. The silver dress she wore showed off her curves and her hair was a vivid flag of colour against the pale fabric. Seated on the barstool, her sleek legs were shown off to maximum advantage.

Three years ago he'd felt nothing except anger and disgust for Gemma and he'd hardly thought of her in the intervening years. So what the hell had changed? Why could he not stop noticing every detail about her? Especially given that it was clear that nothing had changed—she still hankered after Moreau.

He gave a grim smile when she jumped as he stopped beside her.

"Angelo! I thought you were—"

"Busy?" he finished, and gave Moreau a cool nod.

"Well…yes."

"I sorted the problem out and came back to finish our conversation."

"Oh." Her eyes went round. She glanced in Moreau's direction.

Trying to work out how to dump the Frenchman, Angelo suspected.

"Another vodka?" Moreau offered.

Vodka? Angelo narrowed his gaze. A flush rose in her cheeks. *Guilt.* "I thought you didn't drink much of the hard stuff any more? In fact, I seem to remember mention of a hot drink in a coffee shop after I left you earlier."

"Gemma is of age," Moreau interjected. "She can drink whatever she desires."

"I told her to stay away from you." Angelo shot the Frenchman a killing look. Then he said to Gemma, "What the hell does it matter? Have another goddamned vodka with him."

Deeply disappointed he turned and walked away. He told himself he didn't care what she did. Gemma Allen was bad news. A liar. A faithless little cheat. The anger she'd ultimately caused him three years ago had not been worth the pleasure she'd given him in bed.

And she hadn't changed. The sooner he put her out of mind the better.

"Angelo…"

His long, angry strides had already carried him out

the bar, across the entertainment complex and he was headed for the lobby to the elevators that would take him to his penthouse.

"What?" He swung around, glaring down at her as a bolt of sensation shook him as she caught his sleeve. He didn't want this attraction. Not to this woman.

She released him. "Forget it."

"No, you're here now. So talk."

"I wanted to explain why I had a drink with Jean-Paul."

Her eyes were wide and dark. Gentle and pleading. He looked past her, clenching his jaw. All she wanted was his help to regain her memory. Nothing more. Better he remember that. "Drink with whom you please."

"I wanted to find out if he knew anything about the thirty thousand—"

"Forget about trying to find out what happened to the damned money. It's gone. Put your stupidity behind you. So you have some debt, so what? You're young, you can work it off." A pause, then he added softly, "On your back if need be."

Gemma's expression changed. He saw the fury, the darkness in her eyes as she registered the taunt. Her hand came up. She swung wildly. Angelo ducked, she missed. A glass vase from the glass table beside the elevator crashed to the ground. A party of guests took one horrified look at them and hurried past. Gemma barely noticed. Angelo knew he should rush after them, offer them a free night, gambling chips. Damage control.

But he didn't.

Right now Gemma had his full attention.

"How dare you?" She hissed. "How dare you say that, you…you…"

"Gorilla? Neanderthal?" Behind him the elevator opened. He took a deft step backward. "Who knows, I might even be convinced to consider taking you back to my bed and if you're very, very good—maybe I'll help clear that debt." And he hit the button for the roof garden.

She rushed forward, balling her fists and swung again. "I wouldn't sleep with you if you were the last—"

"Neanderthal in the world?" he finished with a hard laugh, and caught her flailing hands. "You might not be so lucky then. You've done it before, why the scruples now?"

He felt her stiffen with outrage. He secured her arms behind her back and pulled her up against him and his mouth slanted across hers.

She tensed.

The elevator shot upward. As his tongue delved into her mouth, Angelo felt her give and lean into him and the familiar arousal shafted through his lower body.

How could he have forgotten how soft her skin was? How full of life her red hair was? Or the little moaning noises she made into his mouth as she pressed against him? He couldn't remember her feeling…tasting…this good.

Hell, so maybe he had amnesia, too.

Distantly he heard the ping of the elevator door opening and the sound of talking and laughter. The rooftop garden was occupied.

Releasing her hands he pressed the ground-floor button and then they were sinking. Her tongue stroked against his, hot and deliberate. The fire inside went wild. He released her hands and cupped her buttocks, pulling her towards him. She came eagerly, rising on tiptoe, her body soft, melting against him like warm golden honey, and he ached with want.

He was tempted to yank open the bow on that wraparound dress, unfurl her, rub his hand between her legs to check if she was damp enough to take him and slide into her slippery warmth. Only the knowledge of where they were stopped him.

An elevator. *Hell.* Given how annoyed she'd been minutes ago, she'd slap him for sure. Hard. Even if only after he'd driven them both to completion, tasted her satisfied sighs. No, better to take it slow.

Instead he slid his hands up…over the feminine curves of her bottom to her waist and back down again tracing the tiny string of an excuse for underwear she wore. Heard her breath catch…and hold. Taking advantage of her expectancy, he fingered the thong through her dress.

She wriggled against him, and he drove his tongue deep into her mouth, giving her a taste of what he wanted, what he really craved. She arched against him and he felt his erection leap.

The car shuddered to a stop. He lifted his head. "Carry on like that and I'll forget my good intentions. I'll hit the button for my suite. Three steps and we'll be in the dining room. Three minutes and we can both be naked. Is that what you want?"

"No." She shook her head wildly, her face shocked and pale. "I don't want this…you." She stumbled backwards out of the confined space, her hands covering her eyes. "God, what am I *doing?*"

He followed more slowly. Putting an arm around

her shoulder he guided her away from the public lobby. Out of sight. "What we've done many times before?" he said helpfully. Her hands dropped away from her face and she bit her lip, her teeth white against the bee-stung bottom lip as she glared at him. But something in her eyes, a deep agonised confusion made him stretch his hand out. "Hey, it's okay, I know you don't remember. But it doesn't matter."

"It matters." It was a wail. Then her head was back in her hands, her fingers knotting through the long dark red curls. "It matters more than I can tell you."

"It doesn't." He stroked her shoulder and noticed absently that his hand was trembling. "I'll tell you something, it's even better now than it ever was in the past. It's more…I can't explain. But I can't seem to get enough of you. The taste of you, the feel of your body up against mine. I want you, Gemma. Badly."

"Believe me, that's not good." The smile she gave him was wan.

"It will be very good," he promised, "you'll see."

"I can't." Her expression grew resolute. "Angelo, I can't make love to you—"

Irritation twisted inside Angelo. He wanted her. He wasn't accustomed to women saying no. "Why? You want to."

"That's arrogant." *But true.* She was terrified she was going to cave in to his demand. She drew a ragged breath. There was one thing he would understand. "I can't make love with you until my memory returns."

He cursed.

"Who knows," she added, "there might be someone else—"

"Someone so important that you don't remember him?" he sneered. "Someone like Jean-Paul Moreau?"

That only made her expression harden. "That's it. Good night. I'm finished with trying to talk to you. I'm going to bed. Alone."

Six

The ringing of the phone woke Gemma. Any plans she'd harboured to sleep late on Thursday—her day off—fell apart when Mark Lyme, the manager of the entertainment complex, told her that Lucie had come down with a flu-like virus. Immediately Gemma offered to take over some of Lucie's performances and arranged a time to meet with Mark to discuss a suitable program.

The Dionysus was a very different set-up to the Electra Theatre, and it had been years since she'd worked in a bar environment. Most of the day was spent putting together the program with Mark and Denny, another performer, for the first fill-in performance early that evening.

The substitute show was rough and ready but it was enough to satisfy the crowd. They sang a couple of duets, Denny told some jokes and they invited some of tourists to sing along karaoke-style.

Gemma caught a brief glimpse of Angelo in the back of the bar halfway through the evening. He was waiting for her and she found herself accepting his invitation to dinner. At first she fretted that he might try to kiss her…seduce her…but her worries proved to be unfounded. Angelo behaved like the perfect gentleman.

Lying in bed that night, Gemma covered her eyes and moaned out loud. *She was so confused.* Who was the real Angelo Apollonides?

By Friday Lucie's temperature was raging and Dr. Natos, the resort doctor, had prescribed bed and rest.

Gemma and Denny met for another rehearsal. During a brief break, she found Angelo at her elbow, holding two paper cups. "Coffee? I'm sure you could use it."

"What's that saying about not trusting Greeks who come bearing gifts?" She slanted him a provocative glance.

"Hardly a gift. Consider it an apology."

After a moment's pause she took the paper cup. "An apology?"

He looked abashed. "For my behaviour the other night. I should have apologised over dinner yesterday. But I didn't."

"Oh." She took a sip. It was strong and sweet and pungent.

He frowned. "I'm confused."

That made two of them! She slanted him a wary glance. "Why?"

"I had no intention of having anything to do with you. But I keep thinking you've changed. Then something happens—like seeing you with Jean-Paul—and I think I'm wrong. You're still the same." He raked his fingers through his golden hair. "Have you changed?"

She shut her eyes. *God.* How on earth was she supposed to respond to that? Not honestly. It was too late for that. She had to soldier on. And then there was the fact that she wasn't ready to face the rage and scorn in his eyes when he discovered her treachery. Not yet.

She'd tell him when she was about to leave. When her contract had ended. And she had uncovered the truth about Mandy. Whatever that might be.

He waved a hand. "Forget it. That's a stupid question. Sit down, you could probably use the break."

Gemma followed him dragging her feet as he led her to the cluster of seating in a small lobby.

His cell phone rang. Fishing it out his pocket, he studied the caller ID. "My mother," he said. "Excuse me."

Angelo could feel Gemma's eyes resting on him as he responded to his mother's well wishes. He listened with half an ear to a story about the car her latest husband had bought, laughed when expected. Conscious of keeping Gemma waiting, he cut the conversation short.

"For a playboy, you have a good relationship with your mother," Gemma said, her eyes curious.

He didn't rise to the bait. "Even playboys have mothers. And, despite all the wealth in the world, her life has not been easy," he answered guardedly. "She fell pregnant with me when she was very young. The man abandoned her. I never met him."

Not *my father,* but *the man,* Gemma noticed.

"Oh."

It must have been hell for a young boy.

"So is today your birthday?"

"Yes—I'm blessed with two celebrations in one month. Last week it was my name day."

"Name day? What's that?"

"A day all people bearing the name of a particular saint celebrate. So on the eighth of November anyone called Angelo celebrates. My mother thought I was an angel when I was born." He gave her a sardonic smile.

She laughed. "Did you get gifts?"

"Most people simply called to send greetings—that's what my cousins, Tariq, Zac and Katy did. My mother sent a gift. Some of the villagers who've known me all my life baked for me."

"O-kay." She suppressed a smile. From what she'd seen of him so far, he'd struck her as a jet-set prince. "I didn't have you pegged for the kind of guy who received home baking."

"I love home baking. But you didn't—too fattening, you said. In fact, you hardly used to eat at all. Your appetite is better now. You've stopped all those diet pills." He gave her a frank, appreciative look. "Now that I think about it, you've picked up a couple of pounds. It suits you. Makes you sexier than ever."

The air sizzled between them.

When she saw Mark waving, Gemma wanted to swear. Angelo had been opening up. She drained the cup and threw it in a trash can. "I have to go," she said to Angelo.

"I'll see you later." He gave her a wry smile. "And I

won't try to seduce you. At least not until your memory returns—unless you ask me very nicely."

That night Gemma and Denny delivered a far more polished show. Her own Friday night show in the Electra Theatre followed, and Gemma returned to her unit exhausted but more than satisfied with how the evening had gone. Kicking off her shoes, she switched on the kettle and made for the loveseat in the sitting area.

The knock on the door came as a total surprise. More surprise followed when the handle rattled and Angelo walked in, clad in dark trousers and a white dress shirt with black snaps. "You've forgotten to lock your door."

"Good evening," she said. "Shouldn't you be partying?" Surely there was no shortage of supermodels or starlets who he could've flown in to help him celebrate.

His gaze went past her to the bare table and neat kitchenette. "I take it you haven't had a chance to eat since your show?"

"No." She liked to wind down first. Then realization dawned. "I'm not having dinner with you. I'm tired."

"You need to eat."

"It's too late to go out."

"Who said anything about going out? We can eat right here, have a picnic on the bed, just like old times. I've ordered some of your favourites from room service. Bollinger, caviar, some crackers." He flashed her a triumphant smile, his teeth white and even against his tanned skin. "And you can't refuse—it's my birthday."

Her favourites.

Mandy's favourites. Suddenly she was wide-awake

and very, very edgy. A picnic on a double bed with Angelo sounded lethal. Even more dangerous than going to dinner with him in one of the resort's restaurants. Given her deception, spending time here in this small, intimate space would be stupid. "I'd rather go out."

Her unease was interrupted by another knock, softer this time.

Angelo's gaze locked with hers. "Too late. Dinner has arrived. No need to do anything. Just relax and enjoy. Nothing is going to happen between us. Not until your memory returns. I promised, remember? And I don't break my word."

But she had no intention of keeping hers.

There would be no return of her rogue memory. *Damn.* How had it ever gotten to the stage that Angelo Apollonides was starting to look like he had more honour than she did?

In the end, Angelo's impromptu birthday supper proved to be a lot of fun. They sat thigh to thigh on the loveseat and ate gourmet food off utilitarian white crockery.

Gemma was under no illusion that Angelo had set out to make her relax. And it was working. She found herself laughing at a story he told about capsizing a catamaran—and liking him more and more as the evening wore on.

On some level a hum of awareness vibrated between them. But it never surfaced enough to make Gemma jumpy and set her on edge. She believed Angelo's promise that he would not try make love to her…and she allowed herself to chill out.

At last the meal was finished. Even the rich chocolate cake, with a single candle on it that Angelo had blown out.

And, seeing that she had no gift, Gemma had insisted on singing "Happy Birthday." For the first time she had seen Angelo flush awkwardly.

After she'd finished giggling at his embarrassment, she'd risen to make coffee and Angelo had followed to help. Only to discover that tiny kitchen area was too cramped for two. So he settled for propping himself up against the counter and watching her prepare the blend. When the coffee was ready, she bustled around, tidying up and they chatted drinking the rich dark brew.

The mug clattered on the countertop as he set it down. When he commented, "Your hair suits you like it is now." She turned from packing away the crockery she'd rinsed off to smile at him, only to find him holding the framed photo of Mandy with their parents.

Gemma's heart came to a standstill. And then it started to race. After the rush of adrenaline came relief. Now he would discover the truth. With a shock Gemma realised that she wanted this masquerade to end. She was not cut out for deception.

His glance shifted between the photo and Gemma. "This must have been taken around the time I—" he hesitated "—knew you."

Her eyes narrowed. He hadn't realised the truth. He'd put the small external differences between her and Mandy down to the passing of time and superficial changes. As his gaze lingered on her, Gemma suspected he was considering the changes that lay below the all-covering jeans and shirt. As he'd noticed, she'd never been as thin as Mandy.

His eyes kindled an urge within her. The flame flickered, danced. Slowly. Sensuously. A womanly desire that refused to be banished.

"I like the curls more than the straight style you wore back then." He glanced down at the photo and back to her and his mouth softened into a smile that she suspected was supposed to melt her innards.

A hint of annoyance doused the desire. How could he not tell the difference between her and Mandy? Suddenly, perversely, she wanted to be found out. "My hair has always been wild," she said, a little tersely. "Curls are much less work."

"So why straighten it?"

She shrugged. "That was the fashion then."

"And you always do as fashion dictates, do you, Gemma?" Suddenly there was an edge in his voice. An edge she didn't understand.

"Excuse me?"

But his attention had returned to the frame cupped in his hands. "Are these your parents?"

"Yes." Gemma moved closer until she could also see the three figures in the photo. Dad was staring sideways at Mandy, while Mum smiled into the camera.

"Your mother's pretty. I can see her resemblance to you—and where the red hair comes from."

"Her name is Beth. She's really easygoing, despite the red hair." Yet despite Mum's normal placidity she'd been vocal in her opposition to Gemma coming back to Strathmos to confront Angelo. Mum had been worried, had begged Gemma to leave the past behind. But Gemma couldn't. She *had* to know…

"And your father looks so proud of you. Who's your mother smiling at?"

Gemma closed her eyes as a sharp burst of memory slivered through her of that sunny day in her parents' suburban garden against the foot of Pigeon Mountain in Auckland. She could remember the scent of the damask roses. She could feel the warmth of the sun on her back. She could remember Mandy laughing—

"I don't remember," she said tonelessly.

Something in her eyes must have alerted him to her confusion and pain because he came swiftly towards her. "Hell, of course you don't. And I'm a stupid idiot to ask such questions."

He was so close that Gemma could smell the scent of his skin overlaid with a tangy aftershave. A hint of amber, of musk…and something else.

Arousal.

A chill shot through her. No! She scuttled backward and collided with a chair jutting out from under the bench top and would have tripped if Angelo's hand hadn't shot out and stopped her from falling.

"Hey!" He yanked her upright. "Are you okay?"

His eyes were a rich turquoise, the colour of the sun-lit sea with no hint of black or grey. The thick brows above were pulled into a frown and Gemma read concern.

She could almost believe—

Damn! She broke free with a sharp twist. She recognized the sensation that unexpectedly flooded her. Recognized its warmth, its seductive danger—and it scared her spitless.

She swallowed, her mouth dry.

She'd been convinced that her hatred would fortify her against this attraction, like a talisman against evil.

So how was she supposed to deal with an Angelo she was beginning to like? Underneath the playboy exterior lay a complex man who was so much more than the media portrayed. She was even starting to doubt that he was the selfish manipulative lover Mandy had described.

"Are you okay?" he repeated.

"I'm fine," she said, and gave an elaborate yawn. "Just tired."

He got the hint but after he'd left, she felt more alone than she'd ever felt in her life.

Gemma was surprised when she looked out into the audience on Saturday night to see Angelo seated with a crowd of people at a table in the front of the Electra Theatre. Three women, all beautiful, and two men.

None of them were eating.

They must be here only for the show. She almost stumbled over her next line, recovered and then sang on, trying very hard not to look in their direction again.

She made it through the show without another stumble. By the time she got to the dressing room, Angelo was waiting.

"Come, there are people I want you to meet."

"I'm tired." It was an excuse. A lie. She was too wired to sleep.

In the end she convinced Angelo to let her shower and change and agreed to meet him at his penthouse—a huge space with black leather furniture and modern artwork and an endless expanse of glass that Gemma realised must showcase fabulous seaviews in the daytime.

The crowd turned out to be Angelo's cousins Zac Kyriakos and Tariq bin Rachid al Zayed and three women; Zac's new wife, Pandora, and Zac's sister, Katy, and their cousin, Stacy.

"We thought we'd surprise Angelo," Zac explained. "His birthday needed celebrating."

"You should feel honoured, Angelo," Pandora said darkly, "I braved a helicopter flight for you."

Angelo gave her a hug. "Thank you for coming. All of you."

A late-night meal had been arranged buffet-style on the sideboard. Grilled calamari, prawns on long elegant skewers and oysters on the shell. Spears of asparagus, slivers of capsicum, sticks of cucumber and sliced fruit added colour beside the seafood.

"Help yourself," Angelo told Gemma, setting down a glass of white wine on the low table beside the sofa on which she sat.

"I will." She threw him a smile and he surprised her by leaning over and brushing a kiss across her brow.

"A toast." Zac raised his wineglass. "To Angelo and many more birthdays."

They all echoed it and Angelo reciprocated by lazily raising his glass and proposing a toast to Pandora and Zac. Which led to Pandora suggesting that it was time for another wedding. A horrible silence followed.

"Don't look at me," Tariq grated. "I'm no advertisement for marriage."

Gemma assessed him. He stared back. She detected suspicion in his golden gaze. He was gorgeous in a stern, hawk-eyed kind of way and wore a long, flowing thobe—although his head was bare—that suited his air of command. She couldn't help wondering what had happened with his wife.

After dinner there was a large marzipan-iced cake, with candles for Angelo to blow out. Gemma grinned at him and decided to spare him another rendition of "Happy Birthday."

"Speech, speech," called Pandora. "Zac, *agapi mou,* come and sit." Pandora patted the cushion beside her. She was blonde and beautiful in a wistful kind of way.

Zac landed beside her and, pulling her onto his lap, he growled. "Don't call me *my love* in that fake way."

"Phony was what I said. Not fake." Pandora started to giggle and gave him a look brimming with love and humour, telling Gemma this was a very private joke.

"Ignore them," Katy advised, rolling her eyes to the ceiling. Gemma noticed that Katy had lines of strain around her eyes. "Pandora is the only person I've ever met who can put my overbearing brother in his place." Katy looked around with a frown. "Now, where is Angelo? Ah, getting out of making his speech and catching up with Tariq in the kitchen. Look at them, they must be talking about women."

Gemma noticed how close the men stood, both serious, their heads together. "I take it Tariq's marriage is unhappy," she murmured softly.

"They're separated. I think the experience totally put him off women," Katy confided.

Gemma started to wonder what these forthright women would say about her later.

Katy seemed to read her mind. "Relax, we like you. Almost as much as Angelo does. Otherwise you wouldn't be getting the inside gossip."

"Angelo doesn't like me," Gemma protested.

"Mmm…maybe *like* isn't a strong enough word. We're not going to ask what happened between the two of you in the past—"

Pandora clambered off Zac's lap and came to stand beside Gemma. "Except that we hope you had a damn good reason for two-timing—"

"Hush. We agreed that was none of our business."

"It is none of your business," Stacy said, entering the conversation. She glared at the other two women.

Gemma stared at the three of them, bemused.

And then Angelo was beside her. "Are you okay?"

She turned her head. "Shouldn't I be?"

He perched beside her and slung an arm around her shoulder. "My family can be a little overwhelming at times."

Pandora and Katy started to laugh. "Come," said Stacy, "give them a break."

Later Angelo saw her back to her unit. The night was cool but there was no rain. The fact that the wind had died down meant that they could hear the hiss of the sea. "I think your family may have the wrong impression about us…me," Gemma said.

The lamps that edged the walkway shed enough light for her to see his eyebrows jerk up. "Why?"

"They seem to think that we're an item. And Katy didn't even seem worried that we'd broken off in the past. Although, I did detect some reserve from Tariq."

"He thinks I'd be mad to take up with you again."

"Oh?" The image of their heads close together in the kitchen came back to her. "You talked about me?"

"Tariq talked. He thinks you'll betray me again. Break my heart."

Gemma wanted to object. To deny that she'd ever do such a thing. Just in time she remembered that he thought she was Mandy. And Mandy had always been a flirt, a heartbreaker. So she drew a deep, steadying breath and asked, "So what did you say?"

In the shadows she could feel the force of his regard. "That I never loved you, so you never broke my heart. And it won't happen this time around, either."

Seven

Angelo and his family all left Strathmos on Sunday. Gemma heard the beat of the blades of the helicopter departing just after noon, but didn't realise that Angelo had gone until she found the note in the backstage pigeon hole where her mail was delivered.

Back next Sunday. See you then.

That was all. He hadn't even signed it. But she knew without doubt who had sent it.

Later she heard that he'd gone to Athens, that he'd be flying on to the resort at Kalos for a series of hush-hush meetings about a new opportunity he was investigating. Gemma had expected to feel relief at his absence, a cessation of the tension that twisted within her. But instead there was only an unfamiliar emptiness inside her.

Gemma suspected she was headed for heartbreak. Angelo had made it clear last night that there was no chance that he would ever love her. So she'd better take care to guard her hollow heart.

Gemma took one of the bicycles that the resort made available to the staff and guests and cycled down to Nexos, the small fishing village or *xorio,* not far from the resort.

The tables outside the local *taverna* were all taken. Most by locals playing *tavli,* backgammon. At one end, a fashionably dressed couple, clearly from the resort, shared a platter of *mezze* with olives and pita and a selection of spreads. Another young couple sat holding hands across a table. And a pang shot through Gemma.

There was no chance that she and Angelo would ever resemble these lover-like couples.

She turned away from the tables and chairs and wandered into the bakery beside the taverna, spoiling herself to a couple of *tiropites*—triangles of phyllo pastry filled with cheese—and a bottle of mineral water. She wheeled the bicycle across the cobbles and settled herself on the seawall to watch the fishermen spreading the nets in the sun and eat her impromptu lunch.

All around her, village life carried on. Across the road, two elderly widows dressed from head to toe in black were shuffling into the churchyard of the quaint white-washed church with its domed bright blue roof.

The church reminded her of Pandora's talk about weddings yesterday and Tariq's bitterness. Had he loved his wife? Why had his marriage fallen apart?

Of course, love was not strictly necessary for a marriage—or even for a relationship. Angelo had confessed last night that he'd never loved Mandy. What was it with these men?

Then she thought of the loving tenderness Zac demonstrated to Pandora and an ache settled in the region of Gemma's heart.

Unscrewing the top off the mineral water, she took a swig. She doubted Angelo would ever love anyone like that, without reserve. He was so self-contained, he didn't seem to need anyone.

For a fleeting instant Gemma couldn't help wondering whether he was alone now. His little black book would have no shortage of numbers of beautiful women to call on. If he chose to…

The thought depressed her.

Last night he'd made it clear that he was in no danger of falling for her. So much for her wild idea of making him pay.

She'd fantasised about proving to him that he wasn't irresistible to every woman in the world. That she held him in disdain. And she'd contemplated seducing him, making him fall for her, then rejecting him. But now she'd met him and found that he was so far out of her league that her half-baked plans were absurd.

She didn't dare seduce him. Because she suspected that once she'd made love with him, she would never be able to walk away. That she would be marked as Angelo Apollonides's woman for life.

She brushed the crumbs off her fingers and screwed the cap back onto the empty bottle. Sleeping with Angelo was not going to answer all her answers about why Mandy had died. And she could not betray her sister's memory in that fashion. Or risk her heart for a man who would never feel a thing for her.

In a little over a week it would be time to leave Strathmos…and Angelo. And move on. Strathmos was a foreign world, exotic and removed.

Angelo's world.

The empty place in her chest expanded, chilling her. Gemma took a last look at the fishermen on the beach. They looked so unhurried, so content.

Unlike her.

Biting her lip to stop the tears of loneliness that threatened, she rose to her feet and made her way to her bike. She would return to Auckland and get on with her life as her mother had suggested. Perhaps the familiar warmth of her family and friends would bring comfort. Tonight she would call her agent to line up the next gig.

The time had come to lay Mandy to rest.

With Lucie back at work on Monday, Gemma's frenzied schedule returned to normal. Yet she was restless. And her mood was mirrored by the unpredictable weather. Gusts of wind and bursts of hard rain shook the island. Gemma threw herself into her show and a couple of days passed before she had time to draw breath.

Weather allowing, she'd intended to spend her day off on Thursday windsurfing. The morning dawned clear and sunny with enough wind for a good run across the chop. But Gemma's heart wasn't in it. In less than thirty minutes she was back on shore, refusing to admit to herself that windsurfing alone was no longer what she desired.

She missed Angelo.

Blocking out that traitorous thought, she spent the afternoon in the entertainment centre. The resort staff had started erecting a giant Christmas tree and, with nothing else to do, Gemma stayed to help.

It was bittersweet hanging the decorations. It had been a while since she'd celebrated Christmas. Her family had avoided it…Christmas Day had become a time of grief.

As she reached up to hang a silver ball on a branch, her cell phone trilled.

It was Angelo.

Immediately her pulse quickened; the tree seemed greener, the lights around her brighter. For the first time since he'd departed she felt truly alive.

"Missing me?" he asked, humour in his voice.

"Of course not," she lied. "I've been too busy to think about you."

There was a little flat silence. Then he asked what she'd been doing. Gemma told him about the awful weather, the winds and the rain. He laughed a little when she commented that this was not what she expected of life on a Greek island.

"Christmas is coming," he said, "expect more rain."

"Oh, no." Then she told him about the Christmas tree that she was decorating. "It's always strange to see decorations out in November. I can see why your grandfather's tourists came only in the summer months. And I can understand why you've created the casinos and laid on all the entertainment you do. The resort is seething with people."

"Good." He sounded distracted. There was a short silence. Then he said, "I will be back early on Sunday morning. I always attend the Sunday service in the village when I am on Strathmos. Will you come with me this Sunday?"

Spend time with Angelo?

"Of course. But I need to be back for a rehearsal afterward." Even though she knew she was setting herself up for heartbreak by continuing to see him, Gemma simply couldn't resist.

The rest of the week dragged past.

Gemma had just taken a call from her agent on Sunday morning with an offer to sing in a popular Sydney club where Gemma had sung before, when a dull, droning noise interrupted their discussion.

Clutching the cell phone, Gemma rushed out of her unit. A moment later a huge shadow passed over her. Glancing up, she squinted into the sun and made out the dark shape a helicopter.

Angelo was back.

A thread of dark, forbidden excitement shivered through her. "I have to go, Macy."

"Wait, I need to know what—"

"I can't give you an answer. Not now. I'll call you tomorrow." She wasn't aware of Macy's mutterings; all she could think about was that soon she would see Angelo again.

By the time he arrived to collect her, she'd managed to get her pleasure at his return under control.

A rapid glance showed that he was dressed in a beautifully cut designer suit. She wore a smart sleeveless black dress and her hair had been confined into a French braid. Gemma knew she looked elegant and restrained...no hint of her wild excitement showed.

He didn't kiss her, not even a light buss on the cheek. Instead he stared at her for a long moment, his expression unreadable, and her pulse raced. Gemma got the feeling he'd been about to say something momentous.

At last he held out his hand, and said, "Come."

She took it. His clasp was warm and firm, his hand strong. And her heartbeat steadied.

Once they reached the church, she looked around with interest. Despite the white exterior, inside the church, colours ran riot. Just inside the tall double wooden doors, almost a hundred slim white candles flickered. Bowls of bright pink and red cyclamens and a huge vase of crocus added more colour. On the walls, saints with gold-leaf halos looked down on the packed pews.

They found seats near the front. A large woman beckoned to them, gave a very brief smile to Gemma and spoke rapidly to Angelo in Greek as she shifted along the wooden pew. Trapped between the older woman and Angelo, Gemma was very aware of the warmth of his thigh pressing against hers. When the priest appeared, she forced herself to concentrate.

The service was long and unlike any service Gemma had ever attended. Villagers wandered in and out in an ever-changing stream. Children played on the floor beside the windows. And the priest chanted in ancient Greek, while rich incense filled the church.

EDWARD ACCOMANDO
TERRI ACCOMANDO
1607 E WAVERLY CT.
ARLINGTON HEIGHTS, IL 60004

3/89

4156

70-160/719
50016

Pay to the
Order of _____

$ _____

_____ Dollars

Date _____

CLUB50

First Midwest Bank
www.firstmidwest.com

Security features
are included.
Details on back.

For _____

⑆071901604⑆ 0344290601⑈ 4156

MP

Afterwards people spilled out into the churchyard, congregating in small groups under a vine-covered pergola. Angelo kept her close to his side, his arm around her waist. A cat sat on the low wall not far from them; Gemma gave the animal a wary look.

The strange juxtaposition of the exotic resort, the simple church with its ancient ceremonial customs struck Gemma. Had Mandy seen this side of Angelo's world?

Gemma tilted her head to Angelo. "Have I been here before?"

"I asked you to come with me often enough in the past, but you didn't want to."

So Mandy had never been to the church with him. Given her twin's love of sleeping late and her preference for the good life, the refusal made sense. "Do you come often?" Gemma changed the subject.

He propped a foot up on the low wall beside her. The cat saw it as an invitation and came closer, purring and rubbing against his legs. Angelo bent to stroke the appreciative feline. Gemma backed away.

"Are you frightened of cats?" he asked.

"No, allergic," she replied. "I don't need red eyes or a fit of nonstop sneezing."

"Then let's move along." They found a new spot and watched as two girls came to play with the cat. "I come to this church every Sunday morning when I'm on Strathmos. I was baptised here."

"Oh. I didn't know that."

"It's not the kind of thing we usually talk about, is it?" His mouth kinked up. "In fact, we never spoke much at all in the past. I didn't even know you were allergic to cats.

We've talked more in the last couple of weeks than ever before. Maybe it has something to do with the amnesia."

That brought back her deception. Mandy had never been allergic to cats. Gemma certainly didn't want to talk about how she'd deceived him. Even though she knew that she would have to. Soon. On Tuesday she would be giving her last show. And then she'd be leaving. For good.

To distract herself, she asked, "Who was the woman who made space for us in the church?" Then added hastily, to justify her curiosity, "She looked familiar. Does she work at the resort?"

"That's Penelope." He pronounced it Pen-e-lop-i with the stress on the *O.* "You met her, when you were here before. Perhaps your memory is starting to return. You should let Dr. Natos check you out at the resort."

That was the last thing she wanted. "Maybe my head is getting better." He didn't look convinced. "Who is Penelope?" She asked again. "In case we bump into each other—she'd think me rude if I didn't know."

He shot her a strange look. "That didn't worry you much in the past. You never had much time for her. She was my governess when I was a child."

"A governess?" It accentuated the divide between them. She hadn't been deprived, but hers hadn't been an upbringing populated with governesses and servants and limitless privilege.

"Someone had to teach me to read and write. I didn't get sent to school in England until I was ten."

"You went to school in England?" That would account for his flawless English—no hint of an accent, no misuse of idiom.

"Yes, my mother thought it was for the best. My grandfather couldn't sway her."

"Did you enjoy it?"

"Not at first," he admitted. "It was a long way from home. I didn't speak good English. Initially I felt so isolated. I wanted to come home."

"Home? Here? To the resort?"

"No, there was no resort. There used to be a house on the island."

Gemma gave the hill behind the village a sweeping look. "A house?"

"I pulled it down and built the resort on the site of the wreckage."

Something in his voice gave her reason to pause. The tanned skin had stretched tautly across the high, flat cheekbones. He looked remote and ruthless.

Gemma shivered. There was so much she still didn't know about him. And now it was too late. She would be leaving soon.

After they got back to the resort, Gemma hurried to the entertainment centre to help Mark with the Christmas show rehearsal. She wouldn't perform in that. Tomorrow would be her last appearance. In a couple of days, she'd be back in Auckland. And she'd have to put the pieces of her life back together again.

"Gemma." She started when she heard her name called. Mark and Lucie were watching her with quizzical expressions.

"Wakey, wakey," Lucie called. "You look like you're off in dreamworld."

Gemma felt herself flush. Nightmare world, more like. "Okay, where are we?"

"In the Apollodrome," said Lucie with a cheeky smile. "Rehearsing for the Christmas spectacular."

"I remember." Gemma flinched the instant the words left her mouth. Lucie and Mark wouldn't realise the savage irony of that.

"Can you sing the Christmas medley?"

"I don't know the words," Gemma called back. "I'll sing something else to give everyone a chance to do the movements."

"Gemma's not booked to sing in the Christmas Eve spectacular." Angelo's voice broke in as she strode forward. "Stella Argyris will be performing."

Gemma stiffened.

"I asked Gemma if she would stand in for Stella," Mark moved forward and gestured to Gemma to get into position. "Stella's not due to arrive for another ten days but many of the other performers are here. I want to get the show on the road, so to speak."

"I've worked with the divine Stella before," Lucie murmured to Gemma. "She's a cat. A man's kind of woman. She'll be itching to get her claws into our gorgeous Greek boss."

Gemma's heart splintered. "Lucie, hush. He might hear you."

Lucie shrugged. "So what?"

Gemma wished she had a fraction of the other girl's insouciance. "Tomorrow is my last day. I want to leave on a good note."

"Judging by the way he's looking at you, I'd say you've hit the highest note already. Stella's gonna hate you."

Gemma whipped around to see what Lucie was on about and encountered Angelo's intimate gaze. "Hurry up—I've got plans for the afternoon."

Gemma turned scarlet. She launched into "O Holy Night." The instant she started to sing "the stars are brightly shining," she knew she'd made a mistake. She'd always loved this carol on a deep, emotional level, but now as she sang the image that came to mind were the silver-white stars in the sky over Strathmos. Why couldn't she've chosen to sing "Away in a Manager," she wondered frantically, at least that would've had no deep, soul-rending connotations.

Angelo seemed to have turned to stone. He was staring at her like he'd never seen her before.

Gemma's lashes feathered down, blocking him out her line of sight. The next line poured from her, her voice swelling, her throat thickened with emotion and her smoky voice became even more husky than normal. The climax came too soon and by the time the last words left her, Gemma was spent.

There was a moment of silence.

"Wow," Lucie broke it, sounding awed. Gemma opened her eyes and blinked. Behind Lucie, Mark had started to clap and one by one the dancers joined in. Only Angelo stood unmoving. Gemma started to feel a little ridiculous; she clambered down the stairs, off the stage.

Finally, Angelo shook himself. He headed off her escape route. "You sing like an angel."

With shock Gemma realised that his voice was hoarse. As if he'd been as moved as she'd been.

"I love that carol," she said, and thought how trite it sounded.

"You sang 'Happy Birthday' to me the other night, but this…this…is something else." He sounded awed. "To think I never even knew you could sing when you were with me. What the hell else did I not know about you?"

At his words Gemma came crashing back to earth. The magic vanished. She was Gemma Allen. Not the Gemma Allen Angelo believed her to be—that was Mandy—but another creature all together. The tangle of deceit she'd created had spun out of control.

After the rehearsal Angelo and Gemma had a light lunch and after she'd changed, he took her sailing. The afternoon passed in rush of wind and laughter.

That evening the applause after her show was even more fervent than usual. And Gemma knew that the audience had sensed the energy and emotion that the day spent with Angelo had unleashed inside her.

She was aware that this could not go on, would soon be over. She still hadn't phoned back Macy about the offer of work in Sydney. By now the job would be taken. Gemma knew she was living for the moment, until it all came crashing down on her head. As it must.

So when Angelo took her back to his penthouse for a late dinner after the show, she didn't protest. This was it. Her last chance to spend time with Angelo in the bubble that she'd created.

During dinner, they spoke of mundane matters, the candles on the table creating a golden haze around them. But beneath the everyday words, something buzzed, vibrating between them, an inexorable force. By the stillness of his body, the light in his eyes, Gemma knew he was aware of it, too.

Setting his knife and fork down, Angelo said, "I haven't helped you regain your memory at all, have I?" His eyes were dark with emotion. "Your return to Strathmos has been in vain."

She should confess now. But she didn't. She didn't want to extinguish that glow on his face that existed for her alone. She wanted to bask in it—for just a little longer. Once the bubble world was gone, it would be burst forever. There'd be no going back.

"Not in vain," she said finally. "The job has been great. And…I met you." Then she hastily tacked on. "Again."

An unmistakable passion flared in his eyes. He pushed back his chair and stood. "Come here."

Gemma knew what he was asking. If she went, everything would change. A moment of fear flickered in her chest. If she went to him…she would have to accept that she no longer believed he had destroyed Mandy and caused her to self-destruct.

That he was not the utter bastard Mandy had painted. That, for her own reasons, Mandy had lied.

"Come," he said again.

Slowly she rose to her feet and started to move around the dinner table. He met her halfway. Took her hand and dropped down onto the long leather couch and pulled her onto his lap.

Need uncoiled within Angelo. A need to see her smile again, to banish the shadows from her eyes, a need for her to be happy, a need to touch her…a need that grew and grew.

What the hell was happening to him? How could he care so little about Gemma's past betrayal? All he knew was that the whole week he'd been away from her had dragged like a prison sentence.

Experience had taught him that Gemma was treacherous, faithless. One side of him craved her, wanted to believe her promise that Jean-Paul meant nothing to her, wanted to believe it could be different this time… and fought to convince that other, more cynical side of Angelo that she had changed.

Her head was turned away from him. From this angle he could see the rise of her cheekbone, the straight line of her nose. He raised his hand, smoothed the wild tangles back to reveal the soft creamy skin at her neck.

"Ask me to make love to you," he breathed. "So that I don't break my promise to you."

He watched her throat move as she swallowed. When she turned her head, he met her gaze and he read the same desire that consumed him, as strong as a relentless tide.

"Please make love to me, Angelo."

A slow sensation rumbled like liquid thunder in his chest and, leaning forward, he brushed his lips across her silken skin. Her mouth opened. She tasted soft and sweet.

A long time later, she gave a breathy gasp and shifted, so that she knelt across his lap, her body tight and expectant.

His hands came up to her shoulders, dislodged the thin shoestring straps and eased the top of the dress down. She wore no bra. One glance revealed that her breasts were high and firm, the nipples dark and his heart began to pound.

He pulled her up…towards him…took the waiting nipple and surrounding flesh into his mouth. The nipple peaked under the stroke of his tongue.

Angelo pursed his lips, sucked, felt her body jerk and wrapped his arms tightly around her.

Her still-clothed belly moved in slow, insistent motions against him. In one swift movement he peeled the Lycra dress off and revelled in the sensation of her naked skin beneath his hands. He stroked her back, the sleek, rounded globes of her tight buttocks; the piece of stretchy lace that qualified for underwear was no barrier to his touch. His fingers slid beneath the thong.

She was warm and wet and his fingers moved effortlessly in the sleek furrow. He could tell by her ragged breathing that she was hot, that she wanted this as much as he did.

As his fingers moved back and forth, his mouth echoed the rhythm against her breast, until she gasped out loud and he felt the suppressed shudder that shook her.

Then she pushed away.

"I can't take more."

Before he could object, she'd slid off his lap, knelt between his thighs. He felt her fingers at the zipper of his trousers. A rush of want surged through him. He grabbed her head between his hands.

"No."

She tipped her head up, her eyes glazed with emotion.

"Yes."

"No." His control was slipping. He had a turbulent sense that if he let this happen his world would never be the same. That he was poised at a doorway to an undiscovered universe.

He heard the zipper give. Her hands brought him out, hard and potent.

"Gemma."

She ignored his desperate croak, her fingertips soft against his sensitive skin.

Giving in, he flung his head back against the sofa and groaned as she stroked him.

When the warmth of her mouth closed over him, he squeezed his eyes shut at the unbearably sweet heat. *"Gemma!"*

The slow sucking started, driving him to the edge of a dark, unfamiliar abyss where he could hold on no more. Shadows started to dance against his eyelids. His thighs began to tremble and then he was convulsing again and again, trapped in pleasure beyond what he'd ever experienced.

Eight

He carried Gemma through to the bedroom, laid her down on his bed. "My turn," he growled.

He stripped the thong off and started to stroke her with fingers that possessed a magic touch. A fine tension tightened in Gemma's belly. She shifted, the raw silk of the bedcover creating a delicious friction against her back, her thighs.

He touched the little button, her knees came off the cover. She moaned. He moved his fingers and her breath left her. Closing her eyes, she shut out everything. Nothing existed, except this room, this man…and his touch.

And then the heat of his mouth was against her. Slick. Teasing. His tongue probed. She gasped. He licked again. Gemma locked her fingers in his golden hair and pulled him away.

"I can't…"

He lifted his head. His eyes gleamed. "You can."

"I want…more."

He must've understood her incoherent mumbles. There was the sound of foil tearing and a moment later he'd crawled over her, his chest hard and sleek against her taut, aching breasts. Then his mouth was over hers, his tongue hungry and plundering as he took her mouth in a kiss so hot, so wild, that her hips bucked under him. Impatient. Desperate.

His hand closed on her breast. Heat seared through her, stabbing between her legs. She bent her knees up, tilted her hips, hinting, clamouring for more.

Angelo moved against her. She could feel his erection, the blunt tip sliding against her. She was ready for him.

He pushed forward and slid all the way in. Gemma moaned, a hoarse primal sound, as pleasure shafted her. Her arms went round his neck, tightening. And her legs wrapped round him, locking him to her.

There was a moment when he lay utterly still, filling her, and then he pulled back a little, and sank forward again. The friction was intense. The pace ratcheted up.

Gemma's breathing quickened, shallow gasps that sounded overloud in the quiet room.

She squeezed her eyes even more tightly shut, focusing on the friction, the sensation that arced through her, from between her legs, through her belly, to her nipples, to her tongue that slid wildly against his.

There was an instant of darkness, the world went black and then she was shivering into a void of light.

Angelo groaned, and she felt him pulsing deep in-

side her. "Hell, it's never been like that," he muttered
hoarsely. *"Never."*

As his words registered, the brightness faded, and a
shiver of apprehension shook her.

Her final show had arrived. Tonight Gemma wore a
black dress with spaghetti straps that made her dark red
hair appear redder than ever. The low scooped back revealed her carefully cultivated tan and Gemma took her
time applying makeup to emphasize her eyes and lips.
By the time she was finished, she knew she looked good.

Her time on stage passed in a blur. She squinted past
the lights but couldn't locate Angelo at any of the tables.
At last she gave up and tried to concentrate on the words
she was singing, on communicating the meaning of the
song to the audience, but some of the lustre had gone.

She left the stage with a sinking heart. Her time on
Strathmos was over.

On the way to her dressing room, Denny waved and
Gemma gave him a half-hearted smile.

Pushing the door open, her eyes widened at the unexpected sight of Angelo reclining in her dressing room.
Gemma hesitated on the threshold.

He should've looked out of place surrounded by the
heap of glittery clothes that Lucie had abandoned on the
floor. But he didn't. Instead he looked unfairly at ease
as he dwarfed the couch, his long legs stretched out in
front of him.

She averted her eyes from his gold hair and bright,
piercing eyes and the taut body encased in the beautifully fitting dark suit. Warily, she entered the dressing
room and closed the door. "What are you doing here?"

"Waiting for you. Since this morning, you've been impossible to find. I don't intend to let you run out on me tonight."

Last night had been so special…earth shattering… she hadn't been able to face him this morning. She'd needed time alone to come to terms with it.

"I wouldn't have run out on you." They needed to talk. He was going to be furious with her. Her heart clenched at the thought of the coming confrontation.

"Join me for dinner?"

Dark and deep, that voice did stuff to her that should be declared illegal. "Anywhere except your penthouse." She didn't want to make love, it would distract her from what she had to say.

The smile he gave her was irresistible. "*Endaxi*. Okay."

He took her to the Golden Fleece. The decor was rich and warm with exquisitely painted murals on the walls of Jason and the Argonauts performing daring deeds. The high-backed chairs, white table linen and dim lighting, together with the hushed service gave it an outrageously exclusive ambience. As the meal progressed, and the conversation topics remained general, the tension that grasped Gemma started to unwind.

Gemma declined desert in favour of coffee and while they were waiting for it to arrive, she examined a mural depicting Jason with a woman who must be Medea. Angelo followed her gaze. "She was hard work, a sorceress and a witch."

"Yes, but he didn't do right by her. She helped him gain the fleece, he took her back to Corinth and married her. But then decided it was too tough to be married to a woman who was a witch—and a foreigner to boot. So he planned to dump her and marry another woman."

"Except Medea spiked that plan rather dramatically." Angelo's lips curved in a wry smile.

"Poor Glauce," Gemma agreed. "She certainly didn't deserve what she got. Medea's sending a robe steeped in poison as a wedding gift was downright evil."

"You know your Greek mythology pretty well."

"I should do. My father lectured classics. I grew up on the ancient myths. Greek and Roman."

Angelo shot her a surprised stare. "You never told me that."

Uh-oh. Gemma wished she'd kept her mouth shut. Mandy had never been much of a reader, she'd hated what she called "Dad's boring tales."

"So how did you end up a singer?"

"My mother could play the piano reasonably well, so I learned to play, too. I loved to sing, so it wasn't long before I started going for specialist lessons."

"And dancing…what did your mother say about your dance career?"

She drew a deep breath. Should she tell him now? He was smiling at her, his eyes warm. No. In a little while. She wanted just a little longer. "Actually Mum was responsible for that. She was a professional ballet dancer. After w— I…" she broke off at the near give away "…I was born, she opened a dance school and taught lots of little girls instead of performing live—she wanted to spend time with—" *us* "—me. What about you?" She shifted the focus of the conversation to him. "When did you know what you were going to do?"

"On my thirteenth birthday my grandfather took me

out for lunch and told me that one day I would inherit the chain of hotels he owned, and to prepare myself to look after them. My cousin Zac bore the family name, so he would inherit the Kyriakos Shipping Corporation. Tariq was to inherit the oil refineries.

"My grandfather also promised me I'd inherit the three islands he owned—Strathmos, Kalos and Delinos. I'd spent the first years of my life on Strathmos, so I knew it well. After that day I absorbed everything I could about the hospitality industry, about business, that I could lay my hands on."

There was a pause when the coffee arrived. Gemma reflected on the single-mindedness of the man sitting opposite. He'd known what he wanted and gone after it. He been responsible for a large part of his success. There was a lot more to him than the playboy image he projected to the media.

After they'd finished their coffees Angelo walked back to her unit. At the door he took the key from her and unlocked the door before following her in.

Gemma's heart started to knock against her ribs.

"Another coffee?" she asked, desperate for something to do while he stood in her space. Her voice was several notches higher than usual.

"Why not?" Mercifully, he moved away, and Gemma was able to breathe again. He picked up the photo on the bench top and instantly the tension was back, turning her rigid with anxiety. Her breath ragged, she said, "No sugar, right?"

"Black. No sugar."

It figured he wouldn't share her lethally sweet tooth. She emptied sweetener into her coffee and hoped she'd be able to sleep tonight given all the caffeine she was consuming.

"You're holding a cat."

"What?" She stared at him trying to make sense of the comment, to reconcile it with the rising tension that incapacitated her, numbed her ability to think straight.

"In the photo, you're holding a cat." His voice was endlessly patient.

Her brow wrinkled. "Yes, Snuggles."

"You told me you were allergic to cats."

Uh-huh. Gemma stiffened, wary of a trap. "I am," she said slowly. "Snuggles belongs to my parents."

"So why are you holding him? In the churchyard you told me how cats affect you."

Tell him.

She stared at him, her mind went blank. Her tongue felt thick, she scratched for words. "Because he always comes to me. He likes to see me red-eyed and sneezy."

That, at least, was true. Snuggles, the darn cat, had a wicked sense of the misery he caused her. But of course, the real truth was that *she* wasn't holding Snuggles in the photo. Mandy was. And Mandy had no allergy to felines of any description.

The tightrope of lies she was balancing upon became ever more precarious. And when Angelo put the photo down, she said a prayer of thanks and placed the two mugs on the coffee table in front of the loveseat.

Appearing satisfied with her explanation, he sank onto the plump seat. "When are you thinking of leaving?"

"Tomorrow. I'll catch the midday ferry, spend a cou-

ple of days in Athens sightseeing and then I'll fly back
to Auckland."

"It's too soon." His eyes turned to flame. "Come
here."

Tell him. "Angelo—" Gemma backed up at the intent
in his brilliant eyes "—I'm *not* going to sleep with you."

"Who said anything about sleeping?" There was an
intimacy in his gaze that did dangerous things to her
equilibrium. "I just want a kiss."

A kiss…one final kiss… She went into his arms. It
felt like she was coming home. And that created a mael-
strom of emotions churning within her. Guilt. Confusion. Regret that she hadn't met him long before Mandy.

But it didn't stop her responding to him.

When he lifted his head they were both breathing
fast.

"Some kiss," she said.

He didn't smile. Eyes intent, he said, "I have to leave
for Kalos tomorrow. I have a series of meetings there.
Come with me."

She started to shake her head.

"Please, come. You can stay as long as you like. I
don't want you to leave again."

He still thought she was Mandy. But Mandy was
dead. And *she* was alive.

Disturbed by the direction her thoughts were taking,
she rose. She needed to tell him the truth. And leave.
She couldn't allow herself to be tempted to stay. Even
though she wanted to. More than anything.

He grasped her hand and pulled her back. She landed
on his lap. With an embarrassed laugh she struggled to
extricate herself. He wouldn't let her.

Face close to hers, he said, "I want to spend time with you—more than I want you in my bed." There was a hint of bewilderment in his eyes.

And that was when Gemma knew he felt it, too. This strong, enduring bond between them that was turning her life upside down, forcing her to reevaluate who she was and what she wanted from her life.

"Okay, I'll come."

His eyes lit up. He raised her hand to his lips, turned it over and placed a soft, seductive kiss inside her wrist. "You won't regret it."

Gemma gave him a look of disbelief. Of course she was going to regret it. But she couldn't let the chance to spend a few more days with him pass.

Poseidon's Cavern, the resort on Kalos, was magnificent. At the centre of the main resort complex Angelo had installed a giant tank filled with sea creatures and fish. Walking through the lobby, she was drawn to the tank to stare at the rays flapping past the viewing windows.

"This is fantastic." She turned to Angelo. "I've never seen anything like it."

"I brought you here before. Doesn't it stir any memories?"

Gemma's excitement dimmed and she shook her head, hating the lie that she'd trapped herself in.

"Don't worry. Later I'll show the rest of the complex. There's a bar and a restaurant with a fabulous view of the tank. They were designed to feel like part of an underwater grotto. Aside from the theatre and cinemas, there's a water theme park to keep you busy. On the south side of the island we've used the underwater caves in the theme park and we'll take a ride through them tomorrow. It will be a little cool this time of the year, but it's spectacular down there and it's something that we hadn't completed last time you were here."

"That's sounds lovely." But the best part was that it was an experience where she wasn't following in Mandy's footsteps. She wouldn't have to worry about how her twin had reacted.

Not that she was worried about Angelo working the truth out any more. If he hadn't twigged by now that she wasn't Mandy, but her twin sister, it was unlikely that he was going to discover the truth. But she couldn't allow this to go on.

A week, she decided. She'd give herself a week. And then she'd tell him. That night she made love to him with the fervour of the damned. Afterwards he looked at her with a question in his eyes.

When Angelo disappeared the following morning to his all-day meeting, Gemma took one look at the overcast sky, then spent a couple of hours examining the enormous tank inside the resort and reading the plaques about the occupants. Later in the morning she made her way to the heated conservatory pool where she was stunned by the sight of Jean-Paul tanning himself beside a svelte blonde.

"Cherie." He leapt up when he saw her. Gemma turned her head, and the kiss intended for her mouth landed on her cheek.

"Has Apollonides allowed you out your cage, pet?"

His words riled her. "Looks like you've acquired a pet of your own." Gemma gave the blonde a meaningful look.

"She is nothing. I'd drop her like a hot potato if you showed any interest."

His faked heartbroken expression made Gemma glare at him. "You're a wicked man."

"Who loves to do wicked things, remember?" His voice dropped to husky intimacy.

She didn't want to go there. "I don't want to remember."

"Ah, the big fish pays better. How can I blame you?" Jean-Paul sounded philosophical. A waiter materialised at his elbow. "Ah, pull up a lounger for the lady. Gemma, let me order you something to drink and we can catch up on old times."

Gemma wasn't that keen to catch up on old times but she badly wanted to quiz him about Mandy. So she opted for a coffee—and so did Jean-Paul's companion whom he introduced as Birgitte. She turned out to be Swedish and, besides having a wonderful figure, appeared to be thoroughly nice. Gemma couldn't help regretting her *pet* crack. After they'd finished their coffees Birgitte took off to the nearby spa.

"Are you ready for a swim?" Jean-Paul asked.

"In a while."

"I'm sure it won't be long before Apollonides arrives—and he won't like finding you in my company." Jean-Paul looked pleased at the prospect.

Men! Gemma gave a mental headshake. "Angelo doesn't own me. He said I could drink with whom I liked." But apprehension shivered through her.

"If he pays your bills, he owns you. That's how a man thinks."

"How awful." Gemma took the gap he unwittingly provided. "Speaking of bills, after my last encounter with you three years ago my credit card suffered more damage than I expected. I must have gambled more than I'd intended."

"You're calling it *gambling* now?" Moreau shot her guarded look and Gemma's interest picked up. *He knew.*

She gave him an enticing smile. "What would you prefer me to call my little secret, hmm?"

"*Cherie,* better to keep quiet about that. Apollonides might not be happy about your little habit."

So Angelo hadn't known. Or at least that was what Jean-Paul believed. Gemma frowned. That was not the impression Mandy had given Gemma before her death. *I loved him, he ruined me.*

"Did you share my little secret?" It was a shot in the dark. The memory of her sister's wan, sunken face, her listless eyes, her shaking hands still haunted Gemma.

Jean-Paul's gaze sharpened. "Why are you asking me these questions?" His eyes dropped to the shirt over her swimsuit. He pushed the buttons aside.

"Hey, what are you doing? Take your hands off me!"

"Sorry…I thought…it doesn't matter."

But Gemma put it together. "It was you. You introduced her to the drugs that killed her."

"What do you mean *her?* And what are you talking about, saying I introduced *her* to drugs?" Jean-Paul's gaze darted around, examining everyone in the immediate surround.

Gemma realised her indiscretion. She'd nearly given away the fact that she was not the woman he thought she was. She couldn't afford another slip like that. "You were the source, the supplier."

"But, *cherie.*" He stroked his hand along her thigh. "You know all—"

"I don't remember. I had an accident, I lost my memory. So don't *cherie* me." She smacked his hand away. The way he'd touched her chest made sense. "You thought I was wearing a wire. You're scared of being arrested."

A flash of fear flitted through his eyes. "I'll deny it. Everything. You'd be stupid to start this. You've got Apollonides eating out of your hand." He gave an acid laugh. "I never thought I'd see the day that he took you back into his bed. Not after what he saw. He must want you badly. Funny, I didn't think you were that special myself."

Gemma's stomach turned. She felt ill.

Oh, Mandy...how could you?

As Gemma had gotten to know Angelo, she'd come to wonder how Mandy could have cheated on him. Jean-Paul's words made it clear that her sister *had* climbed out of Angelo's arms into the Frenchman's. Angelo was convinced there'd been other men, too. Maybe he was right. And he believed she was Mandy.

Pain twisted deep inside her. Well, she could hardly object. She'd led him to believe she was her twin. She couldn't blame him for that. But she hadn't given a damn about Angelo at the start of her deception, when she'd arrived on Strathmos. She'd believed him to be the bastard who'd gotten Mandy hooked on hard drugs.

But she'd been mistaken.

It wasn't Angelo who started Mandy down her path to destruction...it was Jean-Paul.

Revulsion swept her as Jean-Paul smiled at her, over-familiar and over-expectant. She had to get away from him. He'd ruined her sister's life, caused her death. Mumbling an excuse, Gemma hoisted her tote over her

shoulder and scooted off the lounger, desperate to find
a place where she could be alone to think about what
she had discovered.

One thought kept festering: how could she ever set
her relationship with Angelo right?

Nine

Standing outside one of the boardrooms in the high-tech conference centre, Angelo shook hands with Basil Makrides. "I am pleased you are satisfied with our agreement."

The older man nodded. "I want to spend time with Daphne, with our sons. Too much of my life has been lost on building an empire." There was sadness in his eyes.

Angelo was privy to the tragic situation of Basil's younger son. "I am sorry about Chris. I hope he will recover."

Basil sighed. "We will give him all the support we can. At present he's getting the best care in the world. And Daphne and I will be there at his side when he comes out."

Angelo's step was light as he went to find Gemma. The negotiations with Makrides had ended sooner than he'd expected. He now owned a group of small but exclusive resorts in Australia that he was keen to bring in line with the rest of the Poseidon ventures. He was looking forward to taking a couple of days off and relaxing with Gemma.

She delighted him, enthralled him.

Each day, he grew more intrigued by her, discovered yet another facet of her character. Gemma had changed, more than he could ever believe possible. They meshed in a way that they had never done in the past, in a way that he had never fit with any other woman. He was prepared to let the past go…to start over with her.

He didn't want to think too much about what was happening to him. He simply wanted to enjoy Gemma…her company…and her sexy body.

When he saw her ahead of him, clad in one of the pool's cover-ups, a tote slung over her shoulder, he lengthened his stride.

"Gemma." He snagged her elbow, and she jumped. "Sorry, I didn't mean to startle you."

She turned, her tawny eyes widening when she saw him. Something shifted in the depths, then vanished. "I thought you were busy with a meeting."

"I finished early. And seeing that the squall that threatened this morning has blown away, I wanted to show you the underwater caverns."

Fifteen minutes later, clad in wet suits to minimize the coolness of the subterranean winter water, they each hopped into a giant yellow inner tube that would float them through the honeycomb of tunnels. Because of the cold, there weren't many others in the dimly lit caves, so Gemma pushed off from the wall and scooted across the black water before rebounding off the opposite wall of the tunnel. She gave a squeal of laughter. "This is fun."

"The current will move us along." Angelo's tube bumped into hers, and she laughed again. His gaze lingered on her white smile and pleasure surged within him. "Not scared?"

"Not at all."

"It gets dark a little farther on," he warned.

"Ooh, spooky." She bumped her tube into his, and he rebounded into the wall. Trapped between the cavern wall and her tube, Angelo watched her approach with a wicked smile. Before he could move, she leaned over and scooped some of the dark water into her hand and flung it at him.

Angelo spluttered as the cold spray hit the side of his head. "Is that the way you want to play it?" He growled, using his hands to paddle closer.

"No." Gemma started to giggle helplessly. "Don't wet me more. The water is freezing."

His arm snaked out and hooked around her waist. She shrieked as she slipped off her tube. "Don't dump me in this water, I'm sorry. I won't do it again."

Angelo swept her over the divide between the two tubes. She landed, sprawled across him, her front plastered against his. Instantly he was aware of the softness of her body outlined by the Neoprene suit. The tangle of her wet hair brushed his cheek.

She shifted, twisting away. "My tube!" Her bright

yellow tube bobbed along in the distance, moving fast without a passenger.

"Hold still. You're going to capsize us," he warned, dragging her closer.

She froze. "That's the last thing I want."

"Don't worry, it's only about a metre deep."

"I don't care about the depth. It's the freezing, dark water I want to avoid."

"Be adventurous." Angelo settled her against him. "Live dangerously."

"This is more dangerous than it looks." She sounded breathless.

His arm shifted, he could feel her heart beating wildly. From the exertion? The thrill of the ride? Or something else?

He pulled her closer with one arm, the other holding onto the ring moulded to the tube. "Feel safer now?"

"No," she moaned.

Angelo was smiling when he kissed her. Her lips were cold and wet, but they parted the instant the tip of his tongue stroked hers. The kiss grew wild…deep. He'd never felt this kind of insatiable hunger for a woman before.

Then everything went dark.

He raised his head. "It's the Midnight Bend. We'll round the corner and then there'll be light."

"You think I'm scared?" There was amusement in her voice.

He kissed her again. But she'd moved so he missed the lips he was aiming for in the pitch black, and had to make do with kissing her neck, the softness behind her ears.

"That's so good," she groaned.

He tongued her skin, unbearably aroused.

The tube swung around a curve and they were back in the dim, ghostly light. He pulled away. "Want more?"

"Mmm," she murmured.

This time he made sure he got her lips. The kiss was deep and very, very hungry. Her hand crept up, caressing his nape, then spearing into his hair and pulling him closer still.

Finally he pulled away, breathing hard. "Hold tight," he gasped.

Her hands tightened against his head.

"I mean, hold the tube, hold me. There's a bit of a rapid ahead." He saw her eyes widen, then she was shrieking as the tube started to speed up and go downhill. The tube jerked and shook as the current swept it forward. Angelo braced himself, holding her close against him.

Faster and faster they went.

The last part of the descent was the steepest. Gemma was shaking under the weight of his arm.

"It's okay."

"It's great!"

She gave a whoop of excitement. And that's when he realized she was laughing, that she was high on enjoyment, not shaking with fear. They came careening down the final slide and surfed onto the wide pool at the bottom.

Gemma shifted in his grip, twisted her head around and beamed incandescently up at him. "That was fantastic! Can we do it again?"

And right then Angelo knew why she was different

from every woman he'd ever known. She was so transparent, so intensely warm and joyous.

Gemma was one of a kind.

The next day passed in surges of adrenaline, moments of apprehension and utter pleasure in Angelo's company.

In the morning they spent time feeding the fish in the huge tank and then they went for a walk marked along the island. After lunch, Gemma insisted on trying out ride after ride in the theme park. Protected by the wet suit and high on excitement, Gemma didn't feel cold until several hours later, when Angelo said, "Time to call it a day. We've got guests coming for dinner. You'll like them—the Makrideses are nice people."

Wet and suddenly weary, Gemma allowed Angelo to drape an oversized towel around her and usher her back to the resort.

Back in his penthouse, she stepped gratefully into the shower and let the heat beat against her skin. She lathered her hair, combing the tangles out with her fingers, and afterwards she took her time blow-drying the curls before pinning them up into a sophisticated twist. An easy-to-wear stretchy Lyrca dress followed. A careful application of light makeup and a pair of gold hoop earings, and she was ready to face Angelo and his guests.

She waltzed into the open-plan seating area, only to find the laughing man of earlier gone. Angelo stood with his back to the view over the island, impeccably dressed in black trousers and a black T-shirt, but his jaw was set. "You didn't mention that you had an intimate little tete-a-tete with your former lover at the pool yesterday."

Gemma's heart sank at the coldness in his eyes. She stared at him through her lashes, not knowing quite what to say. She'd wanted to forget about Jean-Paul. Escape. And, to be truthful, she hadn't wanted any mention of the Frenchman to wreck the burgeoning relationship between herself and Angelo.

"Nothing to say? Did you know that Jean-Paul would be here? Is that why you agreed to come?"

"No! Jean-Paul means nothing to me." Angelo's suspicion threw her. She should've expected it. After what Mandy had done, it wasn't surprising. And with that came a further revelation. His opinion mattered because she was starting to have real feelings for him. He was the worst man in the world for her to fall for— Hell, he didn't even know who she was.

The time had come to tell him the truth.

Scanning the piercing eyes, the mouth pulled into a tight line, she knew there would be no forgiveness.

It was way too late.

The elevator pinged, breaking Angelo's fixed, angry stare and Gemma felt weak with relief. Coward, she admonished herself, as he moved fluidly towards the elevator and greeted the man and woman stepping out.

Gemma followed more slowly, wishing the evening was already over. She needed to talk to Angelo alone. For her own peace of mind, she had to come clean. She could delay no longer, however much she wanted to spend time with him.

She forced a smile to her lips as Angelo performed the introductions. She couldn't tell Angelo now, not with his guests here. Later, after they'd gone.

Daphne and Basil Makrides were a reserved couple, both with worry lines around their eyes, though they grew less reserved as the evening wore on. But Angelo remained cool, and Gemma found it increasingly distressing.

Two members of his staff poured them cocktails and served a selection of mezze-style starters. Gemma chatted to Daphne about the resort, about the excitement of the wild ride through the underground caverns, and Daphne smiled.

The conversation moved on to food. Basil and Daphne were well-travelled, and Angelo contributed to the conversation, although Gemma couldn't help being aware of the dark glances he shot her from time to time. She tried to ignore it, chattering gaily and soon all four of them were talking of favourite spots they'd visited.

But the unbearable tension between herself and Angelo caused Gemma's stomach to knot up. When he moved to change the music, she followed him. "I honestly didn't know Jean-Paul would be on the island," Gemma murmured in a low voice that would not reach his guests. "I was surprised when I met him at the pool."

"Maybe not such an accident on Jean-Paul's part."

"For goodness' sake." Gemma rolled her eyes. "He was with a stunning Swede by the name of Birgitte."

Angelo looked surprised.

"Obviously your informant failed to mention that," she said, a touch acerbically. "Although, to be fair, Birgitte did leave to go to the spa for a while. But I also left not long after that. I had no desire to share Jean-Paul's company." She'd stayed only as long as had been necessary to learn what she needed.

Her distaste must have been clear, because his hand covered hers. "I'm sorry."

She jerked under his touch. "Why?"

"For misjudging you. I thought—" There was confusion in his eyes. Pain, and a hint of vulnerability.

He thought she'd been ready to betray him with Jean-Paul. For a second time. *She had to tell him the truth.* A glance in the Makrideses' direction showed her that they were hovering near the dining table. No time now. So she said, "I won't see him again. I promise."

Angelo inclined his head. "Thank you." The liquid voice of Andrea Bocelli swelled through the room. Angelo started to speak, but then he shook his head. "Later."

Later. Apprehension knotted in her stomach. There would be lots to talk about later.

Gemma followed Angelo slowly towards the table where two waiters in waistcoats and bowties were setting out plates with polished-silver covers to keep the food hot.

"Do you have any children?" Gemma asked Daphne after the meal and they'd returned to the comfortable sofas to drink rich coffee from tiny Greek coffee cups. The staff had left, and the four of them were alone.

Daphne stilled. There was an uncomfortable silence and Gemma had the horrible premonition that she'd put her foot squarely in it. Then Daphne replied, "Yes, two sons, Chris and Marco."

Gemma changed the subject and started to talk frantically of the cooling weather and how different it was from Auckland where the weather would now be humid with less than four weeks to go until Christmas.

Gemma chattering on with increasing desperation about Christmas decorations and shopping habits until Daphne said suddenly, "Whenever I try to talk about Chris everyone smiles and talks about something else. It's like he has an unspeakable disease."

"He's ill?" Gemma asked carefully.

"No, not ill, not in the way you mean. He has a… problem."

"Oh." Gemma wasn't sure what more to say. So she said nothing and waited.

"He's in rehabilitation." Daphne named a famous French drug-and-alcohol rehabilitation centre. "It's his third attempt, we're hoping that this time it will work."

Gemma placed her suddenly cold hands over the other woman's. "I'm so sorry."

Daphne's eyes glinted with moisture. "No one lets me talk about it. It's like Chris no longer exists."

"I understand."

"How can you possibly understand?" There was a tinge of anger in the woman's question.

Gemma drew a deep breath. "My sister died of a drug overdose."

Daphne gasped. "I am so sorry. I didn't realise."

"The worst was not realizing she'd been an addict—for some time." Gemma blinked back the familiar tears. "The last couple of months of her life were awful. She self-destructed before my eyes. I was so furious with her." And with her sister's billionaire boyfriend who had gotten her hooked on drugs. *That* anger had been misplaced. "I miss her desperately."

"There are times when I'm so cross with Chris I want to shake him, ask him why he's doing this…and most of all I wonder where Basil and I went wrong." The words burst from Daphne. "We gave him everything we thought he wanted."

"It's not your fault."

Daphne looked at her, her eyes sunken in their sockets, haunted by unhappiness.

"You can't blame yourself. We always try to blame someone in these situations. It's human nature to try find an excuse for terrible things that happen."

She had blamed Angelo. Wrongly. Unfairly. It wasn't his fault Mandy had died. He wasn't the ogre she'd imagined.

Gemma shot him a glance. He was talking to Basil, as if aware of her every move, he glanced up, their eyes tangled…and held. Her heart shifted.

At that moment, Gemma realised she loved him.

She stilled in shock. Then he was in front of her. "Can I get either of you ladies a nightcap?" Gemma and Daphne shook their heads.

"The coffee is good," Daphne said.

Angelo slid into the space beside Gemma on the sofa and his thigh pressed against hers, sending sharp slivers of desire splintering through her. Wrapping his arm around her shoulder, he placed a kiss on her brow. The bold claim took her by surprise, she saw the astonishment in Daphne's eyes as Basil came to stand beside her.

Twenty minutes later the evening was over and, as they walked to the door, Daphne swung around and unexpectedly hugged Gemma.

"Thank you for sharing how you feel about your sister's death, it helped me more than you'll ever know.

At least Chris is still alive, still has a chance to recover. And I've made a decision. I am going to fund a foundation to help warn young people about the dangers of drugs. Basil has spoken about doing something like that in the past. But I was simply too listless to do anything."

Basil threw Gemma a surprised look. It was clear that the topic of Chris and his addiction was not something he was accustomed to his wife discussing. Gemma didn't dare look at Angelo.

Then she told herself he couldn't possibly guess her secret. She forced herself to smile calmly as they said goodbye to the Makrideses.

Angelo locked the elevator with a click. "I didn't know you had a sister."

Gemma's throat closed in apprehension. "Yes."

A frown furrowed his brow. "You told me you were an only child, I never realized you'd lost a sister."

Mandy had denied her existence? Was that what her twin had secretly always wanted? To be the only child, the centre of attention? Did she feel cheated by having to share the limelight with a sister—or worse than that, did she resent the interest that came from being a twin? Something inside Gemma withered at her sister's rejection.

Angelo was speaking again. "What was her name?"

"Mandy." Her answer was terse.

"Is it still painful to talk about her?"

"Very."

"I'm sorry."

His sympathy and tenderness worsened the ache in her heart. His grip on her hand tightened and Gemma's throat tightened. *She loved him.* Her deception pressed in on her. How could she ever tell him? She turned into his arms and lifted her face. His arms tightened around her and his breathing grew heavy.

She wanted to be close to him. Naked. For the last time. Then she'd tell him. And it would all be over.

Ten

In the bedroom they undressed quickly and collapsed onto the bed in a tangle of limbs. A lamp in the corner of the room, between the wide bed and the wall of drawn drapes, cast a pale glow over them.

Angelo moved a little closer. "How did I ever let you go?"

A moment of darkness disturbed the passion that had overtaken her. *He thought she was her sister.* And she had to set him right.

"Angelo—"

His hand trailed across her breast, across the curve, brushing the delicate tip. Gemma sighed as frissons of delight followed beneath his fingertips. She lost track of what she had to say.

Then his tongue came out, probing, tasting the dark

nipple and heat splintered in her belly. Gemma fought a groan as that maddening mouth feasted on her.

He paid homage to the other breast, and when he'd finished Gemma stared at her taut quivering nipples with a sense of shock.

What was it about Angelo that stripped her of all her inhibitions? She wanted him...but there was more. There was a sense of belonging together, a deep-rooted understanding between them that she'd never experienced with anyone else.

It overwhelmed her. It scared her. Because it couldn't possibly survive what she had to confess.

"What are you thinking?" Angelo pulled her against him.

"Nothing." Her voice cracked on the lie. "Nothing," she said again, trying to make it sound convincing to her own ears.

"Then I'll have to give you something to think about." He stretched out a hand to stroke her naked flesh. "You're trembling."

"Yes."

Her breathy reply made Angelo grow harder in anticipation. His every nerve seemed to be on edge, suspended on the razor-edge of pleasure. By contrast, her body was soft, her skin silky under his hand and a wave of tremors shook her.

"Are you all right?"

She nodded, her eyes wide. He paused, determined to take it slow. Then her lips parted, her tongue tip slicked across that luscious lower lip and his control shredded.

A rush of heat seared him. He moved over her, chest

to her breast, his legs sliding along the length of hers, and bent to take that tantalising mouth.

Lower down he was aware of his body pressing into her. Her thighs parted and he tilted his hips forward until no space remained between them.

This close, her eyes were velvety with desire and he was supremely conscious of his strength, the power of his arms braced on each side of her upper arms, the weight of his torso brushing her breasts and the muscles shifting in his thighs. In contrast, she was so feminine, her long legs flexing subtly against him.

Breathing harshly, Angelo lifted his mouth and shifted his weight. Supporting himself on one elbow, he rapidly readied himself with the other hand, hoping he wouldn't erupt before he'd even entered her. The sheath of rubber rolled onto him. She shifted underneath him, tempting, impatient.

As he penetrated her, stretching her, she lay motionless. Finally sheathed deep within her, he lay against her—head bowed, eyes clenched shut—inhaling the sweet fragrance of her skin.

She moved and her inner muscles tightened on him, demanding a response. Pleasure streaked through him and his relentless control frayed. He began the slow sweeps that would take them towards a place he'd never known.

As the pace quickened so did the intensity. His hands cupped her hips, pulling her closer as he drove harder and harder into her. She echoed his ferocity.

When he thought he could take no more, when the pleasure was so great he felt that he would explode if it didn't end, he felt her contract against him, once, twice, and it was enough to tip him over the edge, into the fire that threatened to consume him. And then he pulled her into the curve of his arm, his body warm and relaxed against hers. "Look at me."

Gemma avoided his gaze, simply dropping her head against his chest, nuzzling his skin, breathing in his hot male scent.

She was here now. In his bed. In his life. Did it matter who he thought she was?

She stroked his stomach, let a finger trace the indent between the muscle definition. A wicked temptation called to her. *Kiss him.* He need never know she wasn't Mandy.

After all, if she never told him would he ever learn the truth? Probably not. He'd had many mistresses and none lasted. Their relationship would run its course, too. This sweet madness between them would not last.

But what if it did? What then? Could she keep this secret forever?

No. She didn't want to live with a past that Mandy had already stained with betrayal. She had to tell him. *Now.* While they were immersed in this special, loving glow. Acid ate the back of her throat. She swallowed. He would understand why she'd done what she had. *He had to.*

She pulled away a little, to give herself some breathing space, to gather her courage—and so that she could look into his face, the face she'd come to love so much.

"Hey, come back here, I want to hold you."

Gemma propped a cushion behind her back. "Angelo—" It came out a croak. She tried again. "I need to tell you something." She stroked his cheek with trembling fingers.

"Yes? What's wrong?"

She bit her lip. How…where…to start? She drew a deep breath. "I told you my sister died…"

He nodded.

"She was my twin."

"I'm so sorry. I've heard that twins are very close. It must have been hard. You said her name was Mandy?"

It was Gemma's turn to nod. "She died on Christmas Eve nearly three years ago."

"Three years ago?" Then he snapped his mouth shut.

Gemma could see his resolve not to interrupt, to support her, let her explain. Her love for him swelled.

For the first time she started to hope that he might be able to accept what she was about to tell him.

"Mandy was…well, Mandy. She made me laugh, she loved practical jokes when we were kids. She knew no fear and would try anything." Except Mandy had been terrified of being unpopular. She'd always wanted to be the ahead of the peer group, the first to swear, the first to smoke.

Gemma moved away from him and crossed her legs. "When we were kids we both loved to create shows. I'd sing and she'd dance." She recognized that she was rambling, trying to delay that moment of terrible truth.

"A talented duo. What did Mandy grow up into?"

Gemma hauled in a deep breath, met his gaze squarely. "She became a dancer, an exotic dancer."

Angelo stilled. "So both of you worked as exotic dancers? Did you ever work together? Identical twins… that would've been a card to play." He paused. "Or were you very different from each other?"

"We were nothing alike—even though we looked very similar."

"How similar?"

"Practically identical." The confession was dragged from Gemma. "At school our teachers struggled to tell us apart." Mandy had traded classes with Gemma to avoid those she hated. "And I'm not an exotic dancer, I've only ever sung."

There. She held her breath.

"What do you mean you—" He broke off. A horrible, tense silence followed. He shook his head, his eyes dazed like a fighter reeling from a blow. "What are you saying?"

"You knew Mandy, Angelo," Gemma confirmed. "Three years ago—"

"I knew Gemma." His voice was hard, definite. "Who the hell are you?"

"*I* am Gemma."

"Gemma worked for me, I have a copy of her work permit, her passport, to prove it."

Gemma uncrossed her legs and slung them over the edge of the bed, her back to Angelo. "Mandy didn't have a work permit. She was convicted for shoplifting with a group of friends a teenager. So her application for a work permit was declined."

"*Look at me.*" She heard him move, then he was standing, looming over her. "I want to see your face. We would not give anyone a job without their paperwork being in order."

Gemma took a deep breath. "She had a work permit. She applied for it in my name, without my knowledge. She took my passport and my credit card when she left." And Gemma had never told a soul. When her father surmised that Mandy had been lucky to get a work permit, Gemma had remained silent. She'd been stranded in New Zealand, her career options curtailed— with no chance of working in Australian or Pacific island resorts, furious with her twin, waiting for Mandy to return. She bowed her head, covering her face.

"Didn't you tell the authorities?"

"You have to understand, all our lives we covered for each other. It was a hard habit to break. But I never thought that Mandy would come to any harm, not on a Greek island." Although she had experienced some qualms when Mandy had e-mailed to tell her about the fabulous man she'd hooked up with. Handsome. A billionaire. She'd been even more worried when Mandy had sent her press cuttings and photos of Angelo, whom Gemma had dismissed as a dashing sophisticated playboy. She'd begged Mandy to come home. But Mandy had been in heaven living out her fantasy lifestyle.

Gemma let her hands drop and glanced up at him. "I was more worried that you'd break her heart. You had a reputation as a playboy who went through beautiful woman like a hot knife through butter."

"A lot of that is PR. For show, to attract the jet set." His face darkened. "I'm very generous to my girlfriends. All the women I've been involved with know the score."

Except for her. She'd fallen in love with him. And, at the start, she'd believed Mandy had been in love with him, too. It had never crossed her mind that there'd been someone else in her sister's life.

"So why did you come here?" He flung his arms out wide. "Why the whole elaborate charade of pretending to be your sister?"

"I wanted to get close to you."

He stared at her in disbelief. "You certainly managed that. Did you plan to sleep with me?" There was a cynicism in the lines around his mouth and his bright eyes were dull.

She blinked.

"You did plan this!" He looked at her like she was something nasty.

Gemma swallowed. "In the beginning, I had some stupid half-baked idea that I might seduce you. But I abandoned it." She had to make him believe her. "I thought that you were responsible for Mandy's death."

"What about the amnesia? You told me about a hit-and-run in London. Was that true? Or another lie?"

Gemma looked away and shook her head. "There was no accident. I don't know where Mandy went after leaving here, but by the time she returned to New Zealand she was a pitiful, broken creature. She suffered from moodswings and had muttered wildly about the glamorous man she'd loved…and lost to another woman. I thought that was you."

"Nice to know that you hold me in such high regard," he bit out sardonically. He stalked away, pressed a switch and the wall of curtains started to open. He looked out into the darkness. "When your sister stayed with me, I caught her once using cocaine at a party and I made it clear that I wouldn't tolerate it," he said in a flat monotone. "That if it ever happened again, our relationship was over. She said it was a mistake…that she'd never done it before and wouldn't do it again. I believed her.

"I suspected she had a drinking…problem. I'd tried to convince her that she needed help after she'd had a little too much to drink at a party, stripped her clothes off and started to can-can. She argued that she was fine, it was just a bit of fun…that I was too staid. I broke it off that night, but she was so apologetic, said she wanted another chance. I gave it to her." He turned around, his eyes angry. Unforgiving. "And you thought I was responsible for her addictions? Did she tell you that? Mention my name?"

"No." Gemma felt awful. "I assumed. But I knew she'd had a relationship with you—she was so proud of it."

"So you never read about our affair in the scandal-sheets?" he said sardonically.

Gemma shook her head. "Mandy was in a bad way. We didn't have much time with her once she returned home. She took an overdose and then she was dead."

"Was it deliberate?" His voice softened.

For a wild moment Gemma thought he was about to reach for her, but then his eyes iced over.

Her throat thickened. "I thought so. I thought that you'd driven her away after getting her hooked on drugs, that she coped by turning to the drugs for solace. I thought she didn't want to live without you."

He paced along the length of the window, a dark shape against the night. "No wonder you hated me. No wonder you wanted revenge. But do you have any conception of the kind of danger that you put yourself in? What if I'd been the kind of man you thought?"

"I *had* to do it. She was my twin sister. My other half." And then she realized that was wrong. *He* was her other half. The bond, the empathy, that had been growing between them was stronger than anything she'd ever shared with her sister. She rose to her feet, took a step towards him. "Angelo—"

"Even though she lied to you, stole from you, de-frauded you?" He was angry, she saw. "Mandy used the credit card that you told me you'd mysteriously maxed out and couldn't remember how, didn't she?"

"Yes. But from what you told me, the dates correlate with after she left Kalos, while she must've been with Jean-Paul. And he supplied drugs to her…he admitted that much to me."

Angelo's gaze narrowed. "I'm not having a dealer on my island. I will take care of him. It makes sense. If Mandy no longer had the allowance I gave her at her disposal, then she must have pawned the jewellery I bought her for a fraction of its value." He glared at her. "Why didn't you stop the card when you discovered it missing?"

She shrugged. "I couldn't leave her stranded over-seas with no money if she needed it. I simply never expected her to run up that kind of debt. She knew I'd have to repay it. It must have been for drugs."

"Well, I won't leave *you* stranded." There was a note of finality in his voice. "I will book you a ticket to take you back to New Zealand safely."

It was over. He was dumping her. Gemma lifted her chin. "That is not necessary. I can make my own way home."

"I can't believe what you did." Anger and a mist of complex emotions clouded his gaze.

"I'm sorry," she whispered.

He turned away, stared out into the night. "I told myself you had changed. I thought I had found a woman who was special…one of a kind. But you are even more treacher-ous than your sister. Your betrayal was calculated to—"

"No, I didn't mean—"

"Be silent." He cut her off. Moving to the door, he added, "I will find somewhere to spend the night. By morning I want you gone. And don't return. Because I never want to see you again."

In the slanting morning light Gemma packed her bags, her heart aching, but she had a frightening suspicion that her heartbreak served her right. She'd called reception and been told that a ferry would be leaving in twenty minutes. If she hurried she could catch the boat to the mainland.

Angelo had not come back to the room since their awful confrontation. She'd waited, huddled on his bed, for him to return.

But he hadn't.

The message was clear. She had to accept that it was over. He did not want to see her. That to him her betrayal was worse than Mandy's had been.

Downstairs, the reception lobby was bustling. Gemma waited in an alcove for the shuttle to the ferry to arrive. The mural of a golden-haired sun god driving his fiery horses across the sky brought a bittersweet lump to her throat. She'd ventured too close to the heat and been badly burned.

But she would survive.

"Gemma?"

She turned at the sound of her name and her heart sank when she saw Jean-Paul. He examined her, his eyes searching for she knew not what, while a frown creased his brow.

"What?"

"You are Gemma?" It was the question that only yesterday she would've dreaded.

"Yes, I am Gemma."

"But you are not the woman I—" he paused "—once knew intimately."

Jean-Paul had worked it out. Probably as a result of her slip the other day. She released the breath she hadn't even known she was holding. "No."

"You're a dead ringer for her. She has to be your twin."

Rage surged through the pain. "Dead is what she is. And it's all your fault."

An ugly expression came over his face. "You breathe one word to Apollonides and I'll tell him the truth. That you've been deceiving him, laughing behind his back. You said that you've forgotten the past. That's how you've explained away not knowing things you should."

Behind him Gemma glimpsed the doorman who had offered to call her when the shuttle came, coming towards them. It was time. She rose. "Do your worst, Jean-Paul. Angelo already knows."

And she walked away leaving Jean-Paul staring after her, his jaw slack.

From the hilltop above the resort Angelo watched the ferry pull away, white water churning in its wake. He shoved his hands deeper into the pockets of his windbreaker.

Gemma was gone.

His mouth twisted. He'd told her to leave, and she'd obeyed. So why did he feel no better?

The wind caught at the windbreaker and ruffled at

his hair. He didn't notice. He narrowed his eyes against the sun and followed the course of the ferry until, a long time later, it disappeared from sight.

Then he started down the hill. A police helicopter approached from the mainland, making for the heliport.

Good. The police had organised a search warrant after his tip-off. Angelo couldn't wait for them to search the man's room and arrest Moreau. He suspected it would be a long, long time before the man frequented any resorts.

Just as it would be a long time before *he* forgot about Gemma.

Eleven

It was humid in Auckland in December. Gemma returned to her parents' home after a morning's Christmas shopping with her mother and made for the bathroom clutching the box she'd bought at the pharmacy. In less than five minutes she had the answer she'd dreaded.

"Mum," she staggered out the bathroom. "This is going to be a shock."

"What's wrong, darling?"

"I'm pregnant."

"Are you sure?"

Gemma nodded and held up the indicator stick.

"Oh." Her mother looked like she wanted to say something. Finally she asked, "Do you know who the father is?"

"Of course I do."

"But you're not telling?"

Gemma gave a laugh. To her own ears it sounded hysterical. "I will when I'm ready." She wrapped her arms around her mother. "You shouldn't be so understanding."

Her mother hugged her back. "How can I not be? Do you know how far along you are?"

"Not far at all. I missed a period, that's what clued me in. I've always been so regular."

"Go see your doctor. You may not be pregnant at all. Perhaps your body is just playing tricks on you after the long flight."

"I've been back almost two weeks—it's unlikely to be the flight."

Beth Allen shook her head. "But the pill makes the chance of it happening so remote."

"Except I haven't been on the pill for a while. There was no one in my life, so there seemed little point. He used protection. Something must have gone wrong. I'll go see the doctor, but I doubt it will change things." Deep in her heart Gemma was already sure. "Mum, I should tell you. The father is—" She broke off.

"Yes, darling?"

Gemma swallowed. "It's Angelo Apollonides."

Her mother's hand came up to cover her mouth, but no sound escaped. But her eyes were wide and dismayed as she stared at Gemma. Then she stepped forward and hugged Gemma. "You can tell how it came to pass when you're ready."

They stood like that for a long while, holding one another, and Gemma drew support from her mother's warmth. At last she said, "Thanks, Mum, for your support."

"Your father and I will always be there for you and the baby."

"I know. But I need to you to understand one thing, Mum. Angelo wasn't responsible for what happened to Mandy. It was another guy, Jean-Paul Moreau. I think Mandy loved him, and he rewarded her by making her into an addict. I hope he burns in hell."

"Oh, sweetheart, I have to tell you that is a relief to hear it wasn't your Angelo."

Later Gemma went home to the apartment she'd rented out while she went to Greece. It seemed strange to be living in the middle of the city after the time she'd spent on Strathmos.

Gemma made a pot of weak herbal tea and poured herself a mug. She intended to cut down on caffeine for the next nine months, that meant less tea and coffee.

Taking the mug she made her way to the dining-room table. She lay her hand on her flat stomach and thought about the baby. About the future. And about Angelo.

The phone interrupted her thoughts. It was her agent, thrilled with an offer for Gemma to perform at a brand-new Australian resort.

"It's the chance of a lifetime," Macy was gabbling. "The money is great and it's for six months. You get star billing. You'd be mad to let this pass."

Gemma considered it. The sum would wipe out the debt on her credit card; help her start the baby's life on much more stable footing. She could sublet the apartment while she was gone, that would give her a nest egg. But she couldn't take the job for the full six months. She'd be showing by then and she'd want to slow down.

"Macy, see if they'll do a deal for three months. I'll take that. I'll be ready to start in the new year. But get me the best money that you can."

She set the phone down, feeling a lot better now that she had a plan to get the burden of the debt Mandy had run up under control.

Now she'd have to call Angelo and let him know about the baby. He deserved that much.

Macy called back two days later, ecstatic with the deal she'd managed to secure Gemma. The contract was for four months and would start in the new year, and she'd managed to better the money, as well.

As for telling Angelo about her pregnancy, in the end Gemma's parents convinced her that it would be better to tell Angelo face to face. Her father was quite forceful about it, and was ready to come along, too, until Gemma talked him out of it. But she was pleased to see that he was looking a lot happier. Her pregnancy had given him a new interest in life.

Gemma had argued at first that flying to Strathmos was an expense she couldn't afford, particularly with the costs that the baby would incur, but in the end they'd convinced her.

So a week later Gemma found herself across the world again on Strathmos. She called ahead to make sure Angelo was in residence. The first person Gemma saw when she reached the resort was Lucie.

"Gemma—" the slight blonde threw her arms around her "—you're back."

"Not to stay, I'm looking for Angelo."

Lucie stepped back, her eyes curious. "He's around

somewhere. But it's the Christmas show tomorrow night, you must come watch. Even though Stella Argyris is the star of the show—and she never lets anyone forget it. She's even more of a pain in the butt than I remembered." Lucie rolled her eyes.

"I will." If she was here that long. If Angelo didn't kick her off the island the moment she delivered her news. And that reminded her, she'd need to book accommodation in the village later so that she'd have somewhere to stay for the night. Although, if the worse came to the worse, she had no doubt that Lucie would let her use the sofa in her unit.

"Any idea where I can find Angelo?"

Lucie shook her head. "He was talking to Mark earlier outside Dionysus's—but that was a while ago. Have him paged," she suggested.

"Thanks." Gemma had no intention of forewarning Angelo about her presence.

She wandered around, Angelo wasn't on the overcast beach where the westerly wind blew the sand up in gusts. Nor was he in the entertainment complex, although Mark greeted her eagerly. She didn't catch a glimpse of him in the lobby so she made her way to the casino. The gaming rooms were already occupied by some of the more hardened gamblers and she smiled at the bouncers as she made her way into the Apollo Club, but there was no sign of Angelo there, either.

She'd just about given up, deciding he must be in his penthouse and that she'd have to have herself announced, when she saw him seated in one of the many coffee bars, with a woman who was making every effort to keep his attention, flicking her long dark hair from her face, thrusting her chest forward to show off a superb stretch of cleavage.

Gemma turned away, her heart constricting. What had she expected? He'd told her he intended to forget her, and what better way than with a beautiful woman?

Angelo was gorgeous, wealthy…of course women would throw themselves at him. She'd never expected him to hanker after her. Yet seeing him with someone else hurt. Horribly. She made blindly for the exit. Outside the air was cool, the wintery edge of the wind cutting through her cardigan.

Gemma headed for the entertainment centre. As she rounded a bend, she saw Mark approaching from the opposite direction. She had no desire to talk to anyone so she slipped through a door into the massive Apollo-drome super bowl where the Christmas extravaganza would be held.

She slipped into a seat and fought to blink back the tears that threatened. People came in and out, a couple of guys shifted props across the stage, but in the huge space she remained unnoticed.

It was a while before she gained sufficient control over her emotions to feel up to venturing out. The people had started to buzz in and out and she didn't particularly want to bump into anyone she knew. So she stayed where she was and realised the final dress rehearsal must be about to start. Squinting, she recognised several of the dancers in their workout gear, a couple of the backing singers. Just as she was about to stand to leave, all the lights came up and she saw Angelo walk up the centre aisle.

But he was not alone.

The beautiful brunette clung on to his arm, talking

vivaciously, her fingers tapping against his arm, demanding his attention. Angelo bent his head.

Gemma shrank back and felt a searing stab of jealousy.

When Mark came across the stage, the brunette rose onto her tiptoes, kissed Angelo's cheek and made for the stage stairs. It was then that Gemma realised that this must be Stella Argyris.

Clearly, Angelo already had a new mistress.

She rose clumsily to her feet, intent on getting out of here. She saw Angelo turn as if drawn by some sixth sense and freeze.

Then she was plunging out of the row of red seats, her heart tearing with pain, desperate to get to the exit, to get away from the sight of them…of him.

Why had she come back to Strathmos?

She should have called him, told him about the baby over the phone. She should never have let her parents talk her into doing the right thing.

But her reluctance to lie to herself made her face the truth.

It wasn't because of the baby that she was here. She'd come because she'd hoped that there was a chance to salvage something between them. That Angelo would take one look at her and know that he wanted her forever.

No chance of that. She'd deluded herself. Angelo had already found a new bed partner. Moved on. He wasn't the kind of guy to fall in love with someone like her. So what had she been thinking?

A hand closed around her arm. "I heard you were here, asking for me. What do you want?"

Affronted and upset, she yanked out of Angelo's

grasp. "I made a mistake. I should never have come back." And then she tried to move past him.

He blocked her path, his body broad and intimidating. "So why are you here?"

She shook her head. "It doesn't matter."

His fabulous eyes glinted. "I will decide if it matters. Something brought you a long way back. What?" There was an intensity in his tone that she didn't understand.

She shrugged, ducked around him and started to walk quickly, her head down, intent on getting away from him.

He kept up with her. "We need to talk."

"No, we don't." She rushed down a flight of stairs, her sights fixed on the exit to the Apollodrome. A vision of Stella Argyris kissing him filled her mind. "There's nothing to say."

She reached the exit and broke into a run, desperate to get out of the entertainment complex, to get away from him, before she started to cry.

She could hear his footsteps behind her. She ran faster, dimly aware that people—performers and tourists—were staring at her as she bolted past.

They'd reached the exit doors. Gemma plunged through them, into the salty windy air. She veered away, heading for the pathway to the village.

He caught her arm. "Slow down."

"Let me go."

He ignored her. Pulling her around to face him, he said, "You wanted to see me, now you've nothing to say?"

"Exactly."

"We need to talk."

She stuck her jaw out. "We don't."

"Okay, I'll talk, you can listen. But I suggest we do

this in the privacy of my suite—unless of course you like the idea of public scrutiny."

Gemma looked around. A group of gardeners was staring at them, talking. One laughed and Gemma flushed.

"No, not a good look for the boss to be arguing with his former mistress in public."

Her chest constricted.

"I don't care what people say about me, but I thought it might worry you."

She glanced up. His eyes were hard, his jaw set. Her breath caught. He was so utterly gorgeous. And she loved him desperately…was carrying his baby. She gave in. "Okay, we'll talk."

Except for the addition of a Christmas tree decorated with gold and red balls, his suite was unchanged from the night weeks ago when she'd carried out a vigil waiting for him to return to her. Gemma wasn't sure why she'd expected it to look different. Probably because, for her, everything had changed that night.

And now she carried Angelo's baby.

"Have a seat."

She took her cardigan off, dropped it on the floor beside the sofa and sat. Then gulped when he moved to stand in front of her. "So, tell me why did you come back? What was so important to come all the way across the world?" His eyes were guarded, but she got a sense that his body was wound tight.

She bit her lip. How was he going to react? Would he be angry? See it as an obstruction to his relationship with Stella?

"I'm waiting."

"I'm pregnant."

Whatever he'd expected, clearly, that wasn't it. His head went back, his eyes flaring with shock...and something else.

"Run that by me again?" he said very, very softly.

"I'm pregnant." Tremors of tension shimmered through Gemma as she waited for his reaction.

His eyes narrowed. "You're pregnant. Did you do it deliberately?"

Twelve

"*What?*" Gemma didn't try to hide her shock.

Angelo's handsome features could have been carved out of marble. "Is this your idea of revenge? Your way of punishing me for your belief that I'd caused your sister's death? Did you plan all along to fall into my bed, to get pregnant?"

"*No.*"

His tension uncoiled infinitesimally. "So why *did* you let me make love to you, knowing I thought you were *Mandy?*"

Oh, dear God, this was the one question she could not answer. Not without giving herself away. Irretrievably.

So she said with a touch of mockery, "Because you turn me on. More than any man I've ever met."

His voice held an edge. "Oh, that's the only reason?"

She shrugged. "Well, yes. What more could there be?"

"What more could there be?" he repeated savagely. Then he landed on the arm of the sofa and slid in behind her. "What more could there be?" A feather light kiss landed on her cheek. "This…" He pulled her across his lap, angled his head and his tongue stroked across her bottom lip, igniting a well of longing within her. "Someone who turned you on. That's all I was?" There was affront beneath the annoyance.

"Well, that's pretty much why you slept with me, wasn't it?"

"Maybe I thought I'd found my dream woman." His voice was ironic. Before Gemma could respond, his hand slid under her T-shirt, found the bud of her breast. "I was wrong. But we still have this, don't we?"

Gemma shoved his hand away. She felt a tearing ache of loss. He *didn't* love her. He could never love her. "I just wanted to tell you that the baby existed. You have a right to know. I won't even put your name on the birth certificate."

"Why not?"

"You want to be listed as the father?" She'd never expected that.

"Of course. No child of mine will grow up with the slur of *father unknown*."

She took a deep breath. "What will you tell people? What about Stella?"

"Stella?" He frowned, bewilderment clouding his features. "Why are you asking about Stella?"

"I saw you. I saw you kissing her."

The frown deepened and his eyes grew cool. "You saw Stella kissing *me*."

She folded her arms across her breasts. "And I saw

you having an intimate little conversation in the coffee shop," she plunged on.

He shrugged. "Stella wanted something."

Stella wanted something. That was for sure. Stella wanted Angelo Apollonides. "Are you trying to tell me that there is nothing between you and her?"

"That's exactly what I'm telling you."

"That you haven't slept with her since I left?"

"I shouldn't need to answer that. Especially since your only reason for sleeping with me was because I was a warm body." The savagery was back, and his lip curled into a snarl.

Doubts swirled through Gemma. What did Angelo want of her? Did he mean that he hadn't had another woman since she left? And given his reputation, could she believe that?

He was moving away. "And you won't need to worry about other women—because we're getting married."

Gemma froze. "Why should I marry you?"

His eyes grew wary. "I would never knowingly allow a child of mine to be raised with the slur of illegitimacy."

She didn't want Angelo marrying her only for the sake of the baby. "But lots of couples have children without the blessing of marriage."

"Not me." Angelo was unequivocal. "I grew up in a time when the world was more harshly critical. I lived with the sharp edge of the slurs. Even if the world has changed, I don't want that for my child."

Any romantic hopes Gemma may have harboured about his proposal died. He didn't love her, this was all about making sure his child had parents who were married.

* * *

Gemma was still trying to fathom how to react to Angelo's bombshell when they made their way to the Apollodrome for the Christmas Eve show the following evening.

Angelo had insisted Gemma stay in the penthouse, in the spare bedroom. And, with nothing suitable in her luggage, she'd been grateful to Angelo when a box emblazoned with the fancy logo of one of the exclusive boutiques in the lobby arrived at the door.

Opening the box, she glimpsed a fabric that glowed like crystal between layers of tissue paper. The dress was soft and clingy and fitted as though it had been made for her. The fabric changed colour from snowy white through to sparkling silver. A pair of silver heels and a tiny silver bag completed the outfit.

Now, as she glided backstage beside Angelo, Gemma felt anything but pregnant and ungainly.

Until she looked into a pair of enraged jet-black eyes and read the malevolence there.

"Angelo," Stella croaked, "my throat is in agony."

Mark rushed up and paled with dismay. "My God, Stella, you should've told us earlier. The show is sold out, ready to go."

"I didn't want to be a bother." Stella lowered her eyelashes. "I thought it would pass."

Gemma gave the woman a hard stare. She looked stunning, her black sheath made the most of her curves and her makeup hid any pallor that might reveal that she was unwell. But with a throat infection, she would not be able to sing.

"Angelo, maybe if I sit down a little while, it might

ease." Stella's hands fluttered at Angelo's sleeve, but he was already turning away.

"Mark, where's the program?"

It materialized with a flourish. Angelo pulled out a pen. "We'll cancel the solo that Stella was going to do, replace it with an item by Lucie LaVie—I'm sure she'll have a hilarious Santa story to share."

"But—" Stella's eyes widened with horror.

"And Aletha—" Mark named one of the other singers "—has been working as understudy. She can sing 'Oh, Christmas Tree' and 'Kalanda, Kalanda'—" he named the Greek version of "Jingle Bells" "—but that still leaves a hole where Stella was going to sing an encore all by herself, we'll just have to scrap that."

"But I can—" Stella interrupted frantically.

"Gemma," Angelo touched her arm. "Would you very much mind singing 'O Holy Night' as the encore? Please? I know you're not booked for this, that you were expecting to enjoy the performance as a guest. But would you do it? For me?"

She'd do just about anything for him. Singing her favourite carol was a cinch.

"Of course." She didn't dare look in Stella's direction.

"Brilliant idea," Mark said. "Gemma stood in for Stella in several of the early rehearsals."

"Gemma doesn't need to—"

"Stella, don't worry yourself about it. You're ill. I know that you would not have jeopardized such a show unless you were very sick."

Gemma whipped around to stare at Angelo in astonishment. *He knew*. He knew that Stella had been after the limelight and he'd dealt with her ruthlessly.

She shivered, suddenly feeling sorry for the other woman.

"Now, go." It was an order. "You need to be in bed, taking care of that throat so that you're well enough to perform for your next obligation." Even Stella caught the not-very-subtle warning and she slunk away without a word.

"Gemma, you'll need stage makeup." Mark was shepherding her to the dressing room. "Sorry to spoil your evening, you're a sport to help out when you must have been looking forward to watching the show from the front row."

"But what's everyone going to say when they find out they're not seeing Stella? She's a well-known singer. She'll have fans that came to see her."

Mark shrugged. "Too late to worry about that. At least they get to see a spectacular show, better than a cancellation."

In the wings Gemma waited. She'd also be singing a duet with Denny. She watched as a fire-eater gave a spectacular performance juggling torches and a whole lot of stunts that had the crowd gasping, then she and Denny were on.

The next ten minutes passed in a rush, she could barely remember what had happened. On the way off the stage, she passed a group of Christmas elves going on, a Russian troupe of acrobats that had the audience "oohing" and "aahing."

The carols sounded wonderful. Gemma started to relax. The finale came, everyone was on stage and the chorus voices were rising. Gemma felt the performers' excitement mirrored back by the audience.

Her hand brushed her stomach. *Hear that, baby? Next year you'll see the show, too.* So hard to believe.

The choir sashayed off, the dancers did a last sequence and with a wave they were gone. The curtains fell and applause followed.

Then Gemma was on the stage all alone. The audience lay like a vast sea of darkness ahead of her as a single spotlight lit her.

She searched the front row. And found Angelo through the bright beam of the spotlight.

She launched into "O Holy Night." She sang it for him…as he'd requested. No one else existed.

Only Angelo.

Afterwards she felt drained, but curiously exhilarated as clapping swept the showroom. She waved her hands in thanks, smiled and bowed. When she looked for Angelo again, he was gone and her heart sank.

An expectant hush fell over the crowd. Gemma started to walk to the wings, still facing the audience, waving, smiling until her cheeks hurt. The crowd started to buzz.

She turned to see what had caught their attention.

Angelo was on stage, coming towards her, his arms filled with a huge bouquet of red roses.

Joy twisted through her.

And then she remembered. This tribute was meant for Stella. Not her.

Stella's red roses.

Meaningless. Nothing to do with love. Nothing more than a goodwill gesture of appreciation.

Angelo reached her. He held a microphone in one hand. "That was a marvellous performance." The audience erupted into a burst of clapping. "Yesterday, I asked Gemma Allen to be my wife. Now, I'd like you all to celebrate her answer with me."

He held the microphone towards her.

The silence was absolute. The audience waited. Angelo, waited, his body taut.

Gemma gave him a despairing glance. What was she to say? How could she marry a man who took mistresses rather than a wife? A man who didn't—would never—love her?

Then a woman in the front row jumped up. "Say yes, Gemma."

Startled Gemma squinted into the lights. The woman was unfamiliar, blonde. She smiled, gave her a little wave.

"Ignore my mother," Angelo murmured.

"Your mother?"

Her voice boomed out over the microphone. Gemma blushed as the audience tittered. Out of the darkness came an indecipherable bit of advice.

Gemma ignored it.

She knew what she was going to do.

She was going to marry Angelo. For the sake of her baby. And for her sake…because she loved him.

"Yes." Her voice was strong and clear and the crowd whooped.

Then the roses fell from her grasp as Angelo swept her up into his arms, his mouth meeting hers in a kiss that held hunger and a touch of desperation.

Gemma wasn't acting as she grasped his shoulders and gave the best—and most public—performance of her life.

* * *

There was a Christmas party after the show. Lucie came rushing over with a tray of glasses filled with champagne as soon as she and Angelo arrived. Gemma laughed. "You're making me feel quite the celebrity."

"You are! You are! How could you keep—" Lucie flashed a sideways glance at Angelo "—such a secret from me?"

Angelo grinned. "I only asked her to marry me yesterday. I wasn't going to give her a chance to say no."

"Really? You railroaded her in front of all those people. Oh, naughty man."

Even Gemma laughed at Lucie's antics. And Angelo held her close to his side, his grip possessive, his hand heavy on her hip. For a while Gemma started to think that this could work, that even though he didn't love her, her love...and the baby...would be enough to meld them together.

Angelo went to fetch her a drink and Mark materialized at her side. "Your worry that the crowd would be disappointed by Stella's absence was all for nothing. Angelo's proposal gave them a once-in-a-lifetime show."

Gemma smiled at him. "At least the fans weren't disappointed." But it set her thinking. Had Angelo thought of it as a publicity stunt? She didn't think so. Her experience of him revealed an intensely private man, who as much as he liked a gorgeous woman by his side, treated that woman like a goddess. He was far kinder, far more complex than she'd expected.

The Angelo she'd read about in the gossip columns

was not the kind of man who would've married his pregnant mistress, and she struggled a little with the vast dichotomy between the playboy public profile and the complex man she'd come to love.

It wasn't long before he returned. But he wasn't alone. "My mother, Connie."

Gemma's eyes widened as she took in the slim, tanned woman. Connie looked liked she'd just stepped out of a beauty salon. Immaculate. Tanned. Not a hair out of place. And she certainly didn't look old enough to be Angelo's mother.

"Hello." Gemma smiled uncertainly.

"I am thrilled to meet you. Angelo told me all about you."

Gemma shot Angelo a questioning look. How much had he told his mother? Not everything, she hoped.

"I met your sister, once, briefly. The resemblance is remarkable."

So Angelo must have told his mother about her deception. "We were very close—even though we had little in common."

"Except my son."

"Mamma." Angelo's tone was furious. Gemma was too embarrassed to even look at him.

"I'm sorry. I'm sorry." Connie's hand covered her mouth, her nails perfectly manicured. "I can't ever seem to keep my thoughts to myself."

Angelo's eyes were clouded as he said, "But you can try. At least until Gemma gets to know you a little better."

"I'm sorry, Gemma. Forgive me?" Connie's long manicured nails rested against her arm. "Come, let's sit down somewhere, the three of us. You can tell me about the names you are thinking of for the baby."

So Angelo had told his mother about the pregnancy, as well. His mother seemed to have taken it well. No drama about a grandchild ageing her. Gemma let out a sigh of relief. On the plus side it looked like her future mother-in-law was totally without guile.

"Angelo, a glass of champagne for me please, and—" she turned "—what would you like, Gemma?"

"Water would be fine."

"Make it Perrier, my son." When Angelo wound his way into the throng she said, "Tell me about New Zealand. I have never been there. Are the men good-looking?"

Gemma laughed. They chatted for a while, Angelo brought their drinks and joined them for a while before he was dragged away by a staff member to welcome a big spender who had flown in to try out the Apollo Club and heard about the Christmas party.

"I'm thrilled Angelo is getting married. He always said he never would."

"It's the baby—I don't think he would've married me otherwise." What was the point of hiding why Angelo had proposed?

"So you are aware that Angelo is illegitimate?"

"Yes." Gemma reached out to touch Connie's hand. "But you don't have to—"

"I do. You need to understand the man you're marrying." Connie sighed. "His father was a handsome man, an entertainer, a singer of love songs. I fell in love with him. He was charming...a show man. I was eighteen. An heiress. Too sheltered. I became his mistress. Within the first month I was pregnant. The relationship did not last. I came home to Athens, to my disappointed parents.

"My father arranged a marriage for me to Mario Apollonides. To give the baby a name. My father built the house on Strathmos for me and my son and my new husband. The truth was hushed up. But, of course, there were rumours and lots of speculation. Too many people knew about my passion for Angelo's real father. Needless to say, the marriage lasted less than five years. So you see, my dear, why my son would never marry a woman just to give a baby a name."

Gemma stared at Connie. What was Connie telling her? Was there another reason why Angelo had proposed? He'd insisted that no child of his would grow up a bastard. Was Connie mistaken? Why would Angelo lie?

"Nor did my staying secluded on the island work," Connie continued. "Before long, I'd met another man— a business associate of my father, a millionaire. I became his mistress."

"And what of Angelo?"

"He stayed on the island…with his governess. When he was old enough I sent him to an English boarding school to get him out of the fishbowl that Greek society is. My father wanted Angelo to live with him, in Athens. But he already had another boy in his care, Zac. I was afraid that Angelo would grow up in his shadow."

Gemma remembered Angelo speaking of school, of the isolation. "He was a long way from home."

"Yes. It was hard for him, of course, coming from such a prominent family. I was linked through his school years with quite a few high-profile men."

Angelo would've hated that. But it explained his

attraction to glamourous, sophisticated women who wouldn't demand more than he was prepared to give. Emotionally or by way of permanent commitment.

And his love-them-leave-them image was born.

"And being illegitimate made it worse. Once, when he was about six he asked me why I hadn't married his real father. I told him I'd made a mistake, met the wrong man. But that I needed to get married, because society demanded it. He told me that he wouldn't make a mistake like that, he would never marry the wrong person."

Gemma stared at his mother.

So why had Angelo told her he wanted to marry her for the sake of the baby? Angelo was so self-contained, how was she going to find out?

Gemma was no closer to an answer when Christmas Day finally dawned.

By the time she'd dressed, the rain had set in, echoing her pensive mood, bringing back memories of Mandy's tragic death. She made her way through to the kitchen and stopped in astonishment at the sight of Angelo preparing breakfast.

"Merry Christmas." He grinned at her and leaned over to kiss her cheek. He looked so happy and relaxed that her own mood started to lift. "My mother called, she will join us for lunch—that gives us some time alone. The coffee is already on the go and the table has been laid."

They ate a breakfast of thick Greek yogurt and honey and fruit topped off with fried eggs and bacon. Afterwards they took their coffee mugs through to the lounge and settled beside the Christmas lights. Christmas…Gemma closed her eyes and thought briefly of Mandy.

Be happy for me, sister.

When she opened them, the lights on the tree winked at her, as if to say Mandy had heard her plea. *Thank you.*

When she looked up Angelo stood in front of her holding a gaily wrapped parcel. Gemma was relieved that she'd had the foresight to purchase a book on Greek legends for Angelo for Christmas.

She unwrapped his gift and took out the beautiful silk sarong. "It's beautiful," she mouthed.

He tore the wrappings off his gift and a smile lit his face. "I haven't read this. I'll look forward to it."

Then he took a little parcel out his pocket and tossed it to her.

"What's this?"

He shrugged. But his bright eyes were darker than usual and he looked almost hesitant. "Open it."

The removal of the gold paper revealed a black velvet box. Her heart stopped.

"Do you like it?" he asked softly.

Speechless Gemma stared at the elegant ring, a row of baguette diamonds vertically positioned in a channel setting.

"If you don't like it, we can change it."

His voice sounded far away.

Time seemed to hang suspended. Gemma couldn't stop staring at the ring. What if he never grew to love her? How would she survive being married for the sake of his child? Finally she looked up. "I don't think I can do it."

He stiffened and his gaze grew guarded. "What? Marry me?"

"You're only marrying me because of the baby."

"I want to be part of my child's life."

Gemma stared at him. "You're a high-powered businessman, you flit from resort to resort. You don't really want a family to drag you down." She tried to sound reasonable.

Angelo walked to the window. For a long moment he stood staring out. Then he swung around to face her. "I've been thinking about what Basil said. I'm going to delegate a lot of what I do. Family is important. I want to be part of my son's life. I want us to be married, to bring him up together."

"It won't work." She bit her lip. He sounded so convincing.

His gaze sharpened. "What are you frightened of?"

That you'll never love me. God, he was intuitive. "I'm not frightened. I just don't think—"

"—you can do it." He came towards her and took her hands in his. "You've said that already. But I think you're scared. What are you afraid of?"

Gemma swallowed. "Nothing."

"Then why is your pulse erratic." His fingertips stroked the delicate blue-veined skin inside her wrists. "Why is your breathing so shallow?"

"You know why." She watched him from under her eyelashes. "It's this overwhelming attraction between us."

He shook his head. "If that was all it was you wouldn't be trying to back out, you'd be bright-eyed and eager. No, this is something else." He scanned her face.

She could see that razor-sharp mind thinking. Would he guess the truth?

That she loved him?

"Are you worried that I still have you confused with your sister?"

"No." Strangely that didn't worry her at all.

Some of the tension went out of Angelo. "Good. I'm glad we've got that out the way because the two of you are really not alike at all. I knew you had changed. It simply never crossed my mind there were two of you. I thought you were one of a kind. Now, what are you afraid of?"

Gemma swallowed again. "I don't want to be married to someone who—" She broke off.

"Who what?"

Who didn't love her.

That was the simple truth of it. She'd been contemplating marrying one of the most desirable men on the planet. A man who didn't love her. For the sake of her child.

She must be mad.

"Who what?" he prompted again.

"A man who a zillion other woman are going to find as a hot as I do," she replied after a pause made it clear that he would remain silent until she answered.

"Ah—" he stroked her hand "—now it gets interesting. You'd only need to be concerned if those gazillion women interested me," he said quietly.

She thought about what he'd said. Her stomach rolled over. Could he possibly mean… "So why wouldn't you be interested in any of those zillions of woman?"

"Why did you really agree to marry me?"

There was a burning intensity in his question. Their eyes duelled, held. Indecisively, Gemma gazed into his turquoise depths.

"I'm scared," she confessed.

"Of what?"

"That if I tell you, you'll—" She broke off and shook her head. She couldn't bear it if he laughed…or worse, looked at her with pity in his eyes.

"Would it help if I told you why I asked you to marry me?"

"Because of the baby?"

He drew a deep shuddering breath. "Not because of the baby. For me." His grip tightened on her hands. He leaned closer. "After you left, it wasn't the same. My life was empty. I need you to complete me. I love you."

Her breath caught.

His eyes were bright, unguarded. The love shone from them. "The baby was an excuse, a way of getting what I really wanted. You."

Gemma's breath left her in an audible whoosh. Warmth filled her, her body softened, leaning into him. He felt warm and solid against her. Permanent. "I love you, too."

"At last!" He yanked her into his arms. The kiss that landed on her mouth held a touch of desperation.

And she realised that Angelo had been nervous. He hadn't been sure of her at all. "I was getting cold feet at the idea of being married to someone who didn't love me."

"And I have to admit I wasn't thrilled at marrying someone who wanted me only for my body. Wench." He sat up and grabbed her hand and slid the ring onto her finger. It fit perfectly.

Gemma giggled. "It could've been worse. I could've told you that I was marrying you for your money. To settle my credit-card debt."

"I knew that wasn't a factor."

"How?"

"The offer of the contract to sing in Australia would have taken care of your debt." He slanted her a look. "That's a resort I've recently acquired. I wasn't intending to let you get too far away. Once I got over the shock of your revelation that you weren't Mandy...and the even bigger shock that I wanted you back. I had to make a plan to get you back."

"I should've known!" Gemma laughed with joy. "I almost turned it down. Because I'd discovered I was pregnant. I wanted to work in New Zealand so I could be close to my parents. But the chance to get rid of that debt was too good."

A kiss landed on the top of her head. "Now we'll spend our honeymoon there and I'll spend the four months I have you under contract overseeing the developments I have planned for those resorts."

She cuddled closer. "And speaking of work. I still want to sing. But something Daphne said struck a chord with me. She's talked about starting a foundation to educate young people about the dangers of drugs. I'd like to get involved with that."

"Do anything you want. I will support your decision."

No longer his way. But their way. Gemma smiled to herself. "I'd like to feel that someone like Mandy could be saved. Or someone like Daphne's son, Chris."

He hugged tightly to him. "You have my support, on one condition: we get married before the new year."

She lifted her face to his, hooked her arm around the back of his head and pulled his mouth down to hers. "Deal!"

* * *

Angelo had one final surprise for Gemma. He flew her parents out to Strathmos for the wedding and watched her stunned delight as they walked into the penthouse to surprise her.

He put himself out to charm her parents. Two nights before the wedding the four of them had dinner in the Golden Fleece and afterwards they strolled down to the Apollo Club.

Later they shared a nightcap in the penthouse. By the time her parents were ready to call it a night, it was ten o'clock. After kissing her mother good-night and giving her father a hug and seeing them to the door, Gemma turned to Angelo with a gleam in her eyes that made his throat tighten and said, "I fancy a long, hot soak."

They wallowed in the huge spa tub in his bathroom. Angelo lounged across from her, his damp hair had darkened to bronze but his eyes were as startling, as vivid, as ever.

"Tired?" Angelo's tone was gentle.

She opened her eyes. His gaze held a tenderness she'd never seen before. "More like lazy. I feel like I never want to get out the water."

He smiled. "Oh, I guarantee you'll want to."

Her heartbeat bumped up. Her skin prickled, every inch of her instantly awake and energized.

"Angelo—"

Under the water his hand slid over her belly. "Our baby."

She smiled at him. "Our baby."

His gaze very intent, he said, "I love you, Gemma. Only ever you."

"I know," she murmured. "And for me there will only ever be you."

His eyes started to smoulder. "I believe you. I know you will never betray me.

"Come." He pulled her over him and water washed around them both at the sudden movement.

Gemma became intensely aware of the supple strength of his chest against her back, the hard length of his erection against her buttocks, ready and waiting.

Her head fell back into the crook of his shoulder where it joined his jaw, uncaring that her hair would be soaked.

When his other hand came up to play with her nipple, locking her in the circle of his arms, Gemma made a frantic, keening noise in the back of her throat and bucked her hips.

Angelo laughed softly in her ear. "More?"

The sound she made was barely coherent. One of his hands left her breast, snaked downward and slipped between her thighs.

There was something so intimate about being spread over Angelo's body, unable to see him, but aware of every arch and muscle of his flesh. She felt surrounded by him. He was under her, his arms around her, and all the while the wild flames licked between her legs.

She started to pant. She closed her eyes, focusing on the desire that burned through her.

When Angelo moved, her eyes snapped open. The next instant he hoisted her up onto the lip of the bath, parted her knees and knelt in front of her. She cried out as he entered her.

Heat ripped through her, wild and ferocious.

He moved again, Gemma's hands closed around his head, her fingers digging into the dark gold hair, and then she felt herself give.

"Angelo!' It was a cry of desperation, of satiation.

Angelo stood at the door of the church he'd been baptised in, waiting for his bride.

Connie, along with her latest husband and Gemma's parents, sat in the front row. From where he stood he could see Penelope dabbing the tears of happiness from her eyes. Tariq sat beside Connie, looking very grave, his white robes flowing behind him.

At the altar stood Zac and Pandora who'd agreed to be *koumbaro* and *koumbara* and crown him and Gemma in the wedding ceremony.

At last Angelo heard the drone of a motor and moved towards the entrance. A white limousine emblazoned with the resort's crest came down the winding road and slowed as it reached the church. He narrowed his eyes against the light, trying to catch a glimpse of Gemma.

The village priest materialized beside him. "It looks like your bride has arrived, my son."

Angelo started to move.

The priest's hand caught his arm. "Wait, let her alight."

The driver came around and opened the door.

One taut, elegant leg appeared. Then the other. Finally his bride emerged in a dress so white it dazzled him. He stepped forward, and barely noticed the priest's hand falling away, all his attention focused on the woman ahead.

She smiled at him and offered him her hand. He took it in both of his and raised it to his lips.

"I love you. I honestly do."

She rewarded him with that radiant smile that he knew would brighten the rest of his life.

* * * * *

STOP PRESS

The wedding of playboy hotelier Angelo Apollonides to songbird Gemma Allen was celebrated on the Greek island of Strathmos. When asked for comment, Apollonides stated that he and his wife would be honeymooning in Australia where he has recently acquired a string of brand-new resorts. "I will be taking it easier in the future, and I intend to learn to delegate and spend time with my wife and family."

Rumour has it that, having shaken off the title of the Most Eligible Bachelor in the Universe, Apollonides intends to waste no time in starting a family.

* * * * *

Don't miss the next BILLIONAIRE HEIRS *story.*
Be sure to pick up
THE DESERT BRIDE OF AL ZAYED
by Tessa Radley,
available from Silhouette Desire
this November.

Silhouette® Romantic Suspense
keeps getting hotter!
Turn the page for a sneak preview of
Wendy Rosnau's latest SPY GAMES *title*
SLEEPING WITH DANGER.

Available November 2007.

Silhouette® Romantic Suspense—
Sparked by Danger, Fueled by Passion!

Melita had been expecting a chaste quick kiss of the generic variety. But this kiss with Sully was the kind that sparked a dying flame to life. The kind of kiss you can't plan for. The kind of kiss memories are built on.

The memory of her murdered lover, Nemo, came to her then and she made a starved little noise in the back of her throat. She raised her arms and threaded her fingers through Sully's hair, pulled him closer. Felt his body settle, then melt into her.

In that instant her hunger for him grew, and his for her. She pressed herself to him with more urgency, and he responded in kind.

Melita came out of her kiss-induced memory of Nemo with a start. "Wait a minute." She pushed Sully away from her. "You bastard!"

She spit two nasty words at him in Greek, then wiped his kiss from her lips.

"I thought you deserved some solid proof that I'm still in one piece." He started for the door. "The clock's ticking, honey. Come on, let's get out of here."

"That's it? You sucker me into kissing you, and that's all you have to say?"

"I'm sorry. How's that?"

He didn't sound sorry in the least. "You're—"

"Getting out of this godforsaken prison cell. Stop whining and let's go."

"Not if I was being shot at sunrise. Go. You deserve whatever you get if you walk out that door."

He turned back. "Freedom is what I'm going to get."

"A second of freedom before the guards in the hall shoot you." She jammed her hands on her hips. "And to think I was worried about you."

"If you're staying behind, it's no skin off my ass."

"Wait! What about our deal?"

"You just said you're not coming. Make up your mind."

"Have you forgotten we need a boat?"

"How could I? You keep harping on it."

"I'm not going without a boat. And those guards out there aren't going to just let you walk out of here. You need me and we need a plan."

"I already have a plan. I'm getting out of here. That's the plan."

"I should have realized that you never intended to take me with you from the very beginning. You're a liar and a coward."

Of everything she had read, there was nothing in Sully Paxton's file that hinted he was a coward, but it was the one word that seemed to register in that one-track mind of his. The look he nailed her with a second later was pure venom.

He came at her so quickly she didn't have time to get out of his way. "You know I'm not a coward."

"Prove it. Give me until dawn. I need one more night to put everything in place before we leave the island."

"You're asking me to stay in this cell one more night…and trust you?"

"Yes."

He snorted. "Yesterday you knew they were planning to harm me, but instead of doing something about it you went to bed and never gave me a second thought. Suppose tonight you do the same. By tomorrow I might damn well be in my grave."

"Okay, I screwed up. I won't do it again." Melita sucked in a ragged breath. "I can't leave this minute. Dawn, Sully. Wait until dawn." When he looked as if he was about to say no, she pleaded, "Please wait for me."

"You're asking a lot. The door's open now. I would be a fool to hang around here and trust that you'll be back."

"What you can trust is that I want off this island as badly as you do, and you're my only hope."

"I must be crazy."

"Is that a yes?"

"Dammit!" He turned his back on her. Swore twice more.

"You won't be sorry."

He turned around. "I already am. How about we seal this new deal?"

He was staring at her lips. Suddenly Melita knew what he expected. "We already sealed it."

"One more. You enjoyed it. Admit it."

"I enjoyed it because I was kissing someone else."

He laughed. "That's a good one."

"It's true. It might have been your lips, but it wasn't you I was kissing."

"If that's your excuse for wanting to kiss me, then—"

"I was kissing Nemo."

"What's a nemo?"

Melita gave Sully a look that clearly told him that he was trespassing on sacred ground. She was about to enforce it with a warning when a voice in the hall jerked them both to attention.

She bolted away from the wall. "Get back in bed. Hurry. I'll be here before dawn."

She didn't reach the door before he snagged her arm, pulled her up against him and planted a kiss on her lips that took her completely by surprise.

When he released her, he said, "If you're confused about who just kissed you, the name's Sully. I'll be here waiting at dawn. Don't be late."

Romantic
SUSPENSE

**Sparked by Danger,
Fueled by Passion.**

Onyxx agent Sully Paxton's only chance of
survival lies in the hands of his enemy's daughter
Melita Krizova. He doesn't know he's a pawn in the
beautiful island girl's own plan for escape. Can
they survive their ruses and their fiery attraction?

*Look for the next installment in the
Spy Games miniseries,*

Sleeping with
Danger

by Wendy Rosnau

Available November 2007 wherever you buy books.

HARLEQUIN®

Mediterranean
NIGHTS™

---

*Not everything is above board
on Alexandra's Dream!*

*Enjoy plenty of secrets, drama and sensuality
in the latest from Mediterranean Nights.*

Coming in November 2007...

BELOW DECK

by

Dorien Kelly

Determined to protect her young son,
widow Mei Lin Wang keeps him hidden
aboard *Alexandra's Dream* under cover of
her job. But life gets extremely complicated
when the ship's security officer, Gideon Dayan,
is piqued by the mystery surrounding this
beautiful, haunted woman....

ATHENA FORCE
Heart-pounding romance and thrilling adventure.

History repeats itself...unless she can stop it.

Investigative reporter Winter Archer is thrown into writing
a biography of Athena Academy's founder. But someone
out there will stop at nothing—not even murder—to
ensure that long-buried secrets remain hidden.

ATHENA FORCE

Will the women of Athena unravel Arachne's powerful
web of blackmail and death...or succumb to their
enemies' deadly secrets?

Look for

VENDETTA
by *Meredith Fletcher*

*Available November
wherever you buy books.*

REQUEST YOUR FREE BOOKS!

2 FREE NOVELS
PLUS 2
FREE GIFTS!

Silhouette®
Desire®

Passionate, Powerful, Provocative!

SDES07

Silhouette Desire

COMING NEXT MONTH

#1831 SECRETS OF THE TYCOON'S BRIDE—
Emilie Rose
The Garrisons
This playboy needs a wife and deems his accountant the perfect
bride-to-be…until her scandalous past is revealed.

#1832 SOLD INTO MARRIAGE—Ann Major
Can a wealthy Texan stick to his end of the bargain when he beds
the very woman he's vowed to blackmail?

#1833 CHRISTMAS IN HIS ROYAL BED—Heidi Betts
A scorned debutante discovers that the prince who hired her is the
same man who wants to make her his royal mistress.

#1834 PLAYBOY'S RUTHLESS PAYBACK—
Laura Wright
No Ring Required
His plan for revenge meant seducing his rival's innocent daughter.
But *is* she as innocent as he thinks?

#1835 THE DESERT BRIDE OF AL ZAYED—
Tessa Radley
Billionaire Heirs
She decided her secret marriage to the sheik must end…just as he
declared the time has come to produce his heir.

#1836 THE BILLIONAIRE WHO BOUGHT CHRISTMAS—
Barbara Dunlop
To save his family's fortune, the billionaire tricked his
grandfather's gold-digging fiancée into marriage. Now he
discovers he's wed the wrong woman!